HER BAD, BAD BOSS

NICOLA MARSH

~IN BED WITH THE BOSS ~

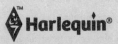

TORONTO NEW YORK LONDON
AMSTERDAM PARIS SYDNEY HAMBURG
STOCKHOLM ATHENS TOKYO MILAN MADRID
PRAGUE WARSAW BUDAPEST AUCKLAND

Recycling programs
for this product may
not exist in your area.

ISBN-13: 978-0-373-52815-8

HER BAD, BAD BOSS
Previously published in the U.K. under the title
WILD NIGHTS WITH HER WICKED BOSS

First North American Publication 2011

Copyright © 2010 by Nicola Marsh

"What now?"

Jade could barely see in the dim street lighting, but she heard the exasperation in Rhys's voice.

"You're ticked off. Not a good start to our working relationship. I don't want to leave things like that—tense, awkward."

She shrugged, feeling more foolish by the minute—a feeling which only increased as she focused on the patch of smooth bronze skin at the base of his throat, where his parka zip didn't go all the way up.

The color of his skin matched her favorite crème caramel dessert…oh, so tempting… A bizarre urge to lick it popped into her mind, and an inane craving to taste him urged her to close the short gap between them and… Just one little lick. Surely that wouldn't be harmful?

Lost in a fanciful haze, she missed the moment he loosened his grip and started running his hands over her upper arms. And though she wore a woolen jumper under her own parka, her skin tingled.

"Doesn't seem too tense now."

She stared at his lips, transfixed. The last thing she needed was a kiss from her boss. What she *wanted*—now, that was a different matter entirely….

NICOLA MARSH has always had a passion for writing and reading. As a youngster, she devoured books when she should have been sleeping, and later kept a diary which could be an epic in itself! These days, when she's not enjoying life with her husband and son in her home city of Melbourne, she's at her computer doing her dream job: creating the romances she loves. Visit Nicola's website at www.nicolamarsh.com for the latest news of her books.

HER BAD,
BAD BOSS

For my original Alaskan lumberjack:
Martin, this one's for you, babe.

CHAPTER ONE

A SCORNED woman needed a new start and Jade had flown from Sydney to Vancouver to get it.

Nothing or no one could stand in her way now.

Just let them try.

She adjusted her suit jacket, smoothed her skirt and approached the reception desk, a black marble semi-circle with Wild Thing emblazoned across the front in large silver letters.

'Hi. I'm Jade Beacham, here to see Mr Cartwright.'

The receptionist, a cool blonde who looked as if she'd stepped off the cover of *Vogue*, pointed to a nearby chair. 'Take a seat. I'll let Mr Cartwright know you're here.'

Ignoring the nerves tumbling through her belly like sugar-overloaded mice, she perched on the edge of a chair, reluctant to sit back for fear of creasing her skirt. Thankfully, she'd had the sense to grab a few of her designer suits before she'd fled her old life, and wearing her fitted sable pinstripe suit, the familiarity of it gave her some stability in a world turned topsy-turvy a few weeks ago.

Her mind drifted for a nanosecond.... Had it only been three weeks since she'd discovered everything, everyone, she believed in had lied to her? That the people she admired the most, the people she loved, were living a sham?

Realising her fingers were cramping from clutching her bag so tight, she deliberately relaxed them, labelling the memories of her former life as a place she didn't want to go; especially not now, when she had to nail this interview.

Her future depended on it.

Better she concentrate on mentally rehearsing her spiel, revising every detail she'd learned about Wild Thing, the world-renowned company famous for its top-end Alaskan wilderness tours.

Thanks to Callum Cartwright, the hot-shot executive who'd interviewed her back home as part of an elaborate screening process, she had a chance at nailing this job.

He'd made it clear that his brother's company Wild Thing accepted very few applicants and expected the best from their employees; if she made it that far.

Well, here she was, ready to impress the heck out of the CEO, land her first job, and take a gigantic step on the road to achieving her dream.

Her dream. Not her parents. Not her ex-fiancé. *Hers.*

'Mr Cartwright will see you now. Through that door.'

The receptionist pointed behind her left shoulder and Jade stood, smiled her thanks, feigning bravado she didn't feel yet eager to take the first step towards rebuilding her life.

Pushing the heavy glass door, she walked into another waiting room facing an endless corridor. She stood for a few minutes, tapping her foot, the silence intimidating her more than she cared to admit. She hadn't flown halfway round the world to be thwarted at this stage, no sir-ree. This job was hers, whatever it took.

As the minutes ticked by her impatience grew. Story of her life, really.

She'd been impatient for as long as she could remember: waiting for the fifty invited guests to arrive at her sixth birthday party at Luna Park, which her parents had hired for the event; waiting for her first pony, first piano, first trip to Disneyland all before the age of ten; waiting for her very own private theatre room with the latest high-tech gadgets by the time she'd hit early teens.

Later, waiting for her first Porsche, her first thoroughbred, and, recently, waiting for the man of her dreams to marry her only to discover he'd turned into her biggest nightmare.

Nah, waiting was for losers. Now she finally had a chance to make things right, to do things differently, to follow her own dreams. Screw waiting. Time to make things happen and that time was now.

Clamping her lips shut on a sigh of exasperation, she strode down the corridor, glancing into empty offices, her patience wearing thinner with every step.

'Can I help you?'

She whirled around, her pulse racing. Being caught snooping in her prospective new work place wasn't a good start. Hoping to bluff her way out of it, she fixed a smile and glanced up.

Rather than her pulse slowing, the sight of the guy in front of her only served to increase its pace.

HOT. H.O.T. flashed across her mind in huge capital letters like the Hollywood sign she'd visited briefly in LA as a kid, when her life had been easy and carefree and mapped out. Shame about the major detour.

He wasn't classically handsome, the planes and angles of his face too angular for that: razor cheekbones, sharp jaw. Exuding barely restrained power, he looked as if he'd stepped off a billboard for executive hotties.

She had a fleeting impression of black hair, brilliant blue eyes, broad chest and navy suit before his face recaptured her attention.

Though she did have a hard time tearing her gaze away from that chest; he would've given Superman a run for his money. Did guys actually have sculpted chests like that? Until now she'd assumed they were a figment of some female comic designer's imagination; some very imaginative, very creative comic designer's imagination.

Those hyperactive mice took to bouncing in her belly again, exacerbating the strange, fluttery feeling she put down to pre-interview jitters. No way could her reaction be remotely hormonal to a guy who would have women falling at his designer-loafered feet with a wink of those baby blues. She knew better than that. Boy, did she know better.

However, the longer the superhero stared at her she knew her racing pulse and somersaulting stomach had little to do with the impending interview and more to do with sexual awareness.

For that was the first word that leapt to mind with this guy: sex. Hot, raunchy, no-holds-barred sex.

As he continued to stare at her with blatant curiosity she suddenly knew how Lois Lane must've felt, all tongue-tied and nervous anticipation at the possibility of being squashed up against a broad wall of muscle covered in a big S.

Surreptitiously swiping her clammy palms down the side of her skirt, she hoped the unexpected heat flooding her body wasn't reflected in her cheeks.

'I was just—'

'Wandering the corridors, snooping around?'

That annoying heat hit her cheeks in an incriminating blush.

'I wasn't snooping. My name's Jade Beacham, I had an interview scheduled twenty-five minutes ago and I was directed to wait in here.'

The babbling wasn't good and, combined with her blush, made her look like a fool.

Something akin to amusement flashed in those too-blue-to-be-legal eyes.

'I'm sure that meant having a seat back there while you wait.'

His tone implied she was a thief about to steal trade secrets as he pointed to a row of chairs, the action stretching his ivory silk shirt tight across his chest.

Oh, boy, that chest...

'You're right. Sorry. Patience has never been one of my virtues.'

Damn, where had that come from? Way to go with first impressions. Mentally cringing and slapping a hand across her mouth, she searched her brain for something sensible to say, coming up a frustrating blank as he continued to stare.

Confident a few deep breaths would refocus her concentration, she took a subtle breath, another, instantly hit by an intoxicating blend of designer cool, warm sunshine and long, decadent nights, the images his aftershave invoked as mind-boggling as the man himself.

Not good. She was here to nail this interview, not swoon over some suit. Besides, her swooning days over any guy were over, remember?

'Here's the deal. I've got a bit of time on my hands, you look like you need to be kept out of trouble. Would you like to know more about your boss?'

His proposition surprised her more than his knockout aftershave. Surely he couldn't be serious? Talk about unprofessional. As for him implying she needed a babysitter, where did he get off?

Shaking her head, she sent him a haughty glare. 'Not interested in gossip. I'm here for an interview, not for you to dish the dirt on your boss.'

He returned her stare, unblinkingly, uncomfortably intense. Damn, why couldn't he be more like mild-mannered Clark Kent? *He* wouldn't be staring at her as if he wanted to rip away her outer layers and delve into her soul.

His eyes bored into hers, an unfathomable expression in their depths as she tried not to squirm under the scrutiny, wishing she'd never started strolling around here. As if she weren't nervous enough, she didn't need some *GQ* model wannabe giving her grief.

After what seemed like an eternity, he waved towards the empty office.

'Why don't you wait in here?'

His deep voice, combined with the brooding stare, had a similar effect on her senses as his tangy aftershave. 'Wow' didn't come close to describing this guy. And he wasn't even wearing a cape!

Anxious for her interview to start, she checked the name on the brass plate on the door. RHYS CARTWRIGHT—CEO.

Okay, so hot guy was being helpful after all, though how ethical was it to wait for the boss in his office? Unless…a strange thought niggled as she gazed from the name plate to the guy. Could Superman be her boss? If so, why was he playing games?

Making a lightning-quick decision, she decided to play along and see what he was up to. She'd come this far; she hadn't gone through the rigours of a screening interview and all the legalities of obtaining work visas and insurance to be turned back now by some nutter, no matter how cute.

She gestured at the name plate. 'You sure this is okay, waiting in his office? Not too presumptuous?'

He smiled, softening the hard plains. 'Relax, you're in capable hands.'

Oh-oh. Not only did he have the Superman persona, he had the killer smile to match. Not fair.

She glanced at his hands, impressed by their strength. Suddenly, a startling image of those hands caressing her skin crossed her mind and she wondered if jet lag had finally caught up with her.

'I'm sure you could handle anything, Mr…?'

Maybe flattery would get her somewhere? She'd try anything to stop him gobbling her up with his eyes.

In response, he closed the door with a resounding thud and she wished the lid on her fertile imagination could be closed as convincingly. Languid warmth stole through her body as she watched him cross the room. He didn't walk, his long legs stalked. Funny, considering she'd imagined them encased in blue Lycra and flying rather than walking.

So much for shutting down her imagination; it was still working a treat.

'As much as I'm enjoying our witty repartee, let's get down to business. Where do you think we should start?'

You can start by unbuttoning my jacket, unzipping my skirt and getting downright dirty.

By the amused look on his face as he sat behind the desk she had a horrifying feeling she'd spoken aloud. It was just like one of those dreams where she walked naked into a roomful of men and they all stared at her. Yeah, this guy had the same look on his face, though rather than making her feel uncomfortable it turned her on.

While she wrestled with her hormones he just sat there and waited for her to speak, looking like God's gift to women. He hadn't answered her question about his identity, so she took his perverse game to the next level.

'Tell me about your boss.'

There. She'd thrown down the gauntlet. No boss would tolerate a prospective employee trying to get a job by such underhanded tactics. Surely he would divulge his identity now and cut to the chase?

'He can be a tyrant—demanding, cranky, uncompromising. He lives for his work and expects nothing less from his employees.' He pronounced it like the company's mission statement.

A test. This bizarre charade had to be some sort of test. If so, she would beat him at his own game and then some.

'Sounds like a real charmer,' she muttered. 'By the way, what's with the secrecy act? What's your name?'

He leaned forward, creating an immediate intimacy. 'Are names important?'

Her traitorous heart beat a staccato rhythm; she didn't know where he was heading with all this and she really wanted to tell him to shove it, but she needed this job. Desperately. Didn't mean she had to kowtow to him.

'You're very confident.'

'It's an integral part of my job,' he said, his gaze twinkling with enjoyment at their sparring, at odds with the steepled fingers resting on his chest, as if he knew something she didn't but held all the power.

She admired his boldness, the way he challenged her with his eyes even if she didn't have a clue what he expected from her or why he was playing some warped game only he knew the rules of.

'As is fraternising with staff.'

Fraternising? What the hell did that mean? If he thought she'd sleep with him to get this job, he could think again.

'I doubt the boss would approve of his employees fraternising,' she said, swallowing to ease her tight throat.

If this job weren't so important she would've gladly told Superman what he could do with his *fraternising*.

'What about with the boss himself?'

His stare trapped her and she knew exactly how the Penguin felt, though it only took her a second to realise she'd mixed up her analogies. Wasn't that Batman? Personally, she'd always been a Superman type of girl and this guy wasn't letting her forget it.

'Jade, I asked you a question.'

He leaned forward and once again that muscular chest strained against the confines of his shirt, threatening to burst out all over the place. She stifled a sigh, thinking it had been ages since she'd seen any seam-ripping action. Like never.

'A pointless question. I'm here to work, not fraternise. Besides, arrogant men can be tiresome and Mr Cartwright sounds like he's right up there with the best of them. He'll be my boss and I'll respect him, but that's about as far as it goes.' There, perhaps her holier-than-thou speech might get a reaction out of him?

To her amazement he laughed, a rich, vibrant sound that sent appreciative thrills down her spine and all her good intentions to ignore him scuttling for cover.

'I like a woman with strong opinions. You're hired.'

'Pardon?'

He leaned back and clasped his hands behind his head, over-confident, overbearing, overwhelming.

'You heard me. Welcome to the firm.'

Jade tried to ignore her heart's erratic reaction as his cocky grin widened. Okay, Superman *was* her new boss. So what if he knocked the socks off her? She just had to remind her clothes not to follow suit.

Annoyed at her physical reaction, she sat straighter. She should be ecstatic she'd got the job, though a small part of her felt cheated. She'd expected a proper interview, a chance to impress with her enthusiasm, not some odd cat-and-mouse game.

'You certainly have an interesting interview technique. Where did you pick it up? Bosses-R-Us?'

He ignored her barb, though his smirk said it all. 'Call me Rhys. We're fairly informal around here.'

His confident tone rankled as much as his smug expression.

'Does that informality extend to harassing prospective employees?'

He frowned, sat forward and placed both hands on the desk, asserting his power.

'What I put you through was a test. Unconventional, I know, even unfair, but I'm the boss and what I say goes.'

She shook her head, resisting the urge to stab a pen through his hand. 'I'm not some crash-test dummy you can experiment with.'

He raised an eyebrow, a hint of a smile tugging at the corners of his mouth. 'No, I guess not.'

An awkward silence lingered before she blurted, 'Look, I'm really keen to start. Do you want to ask me any questions? Check out my credentials?'

She could've bitten her tongue as his gaze briefly flicked over her, checking out *credentials* of a different kind.

For a brief moment she wanted to get the hell out of here, job or not. But she couldn't. The memory of the last confrontation with her parents, the truth of Julian's treachery, hadn't waned. If anything, the truth about her family, her fiancé, motivated her to stick this out, whatever warped game her new boss was playing.

After another lengthy pause, he nodded, curt, dismissive, as he gestured to her résumé sitting on top of the desk.

'You've ticked all the boxes—sense of adventure, love of nature, excellent customer service skills and an advanced certificate in first aid. Looks like you match our job description.'

Grateful play time was over, she nodded.

'I wouldn't have flown all this way if I didn't feel I could be an asset to your company.'

'You haven't listed any formal training apart from a first aid certificate, though Callum was suitably impressed with you at the screening interview.'

He picked up her résumé from the top of his in-tray and flipped through it. 'Impressed enough to get you this far, anyway.'

She blushed, incriminating heat creeping up her neck and into her face. How could she list any formal training if she didn't have any? Pity attending theatre and nightclub opening nights, colour co-ordinating the latest haute couture and shopping for a living couldn't be classed as essential job skills.

'As you can see, one of my career objectives is to become a biologist. This job would be perfect, giving me on-the-job experience and further credits when I apply to enter university as a mature student.'

She sucked in a deep breath, silently praying he bought her spiel. While all of it was true—her dream to be a biologist, her need for on-the-job training, her intention to enrol at uni—all the enthusiasm in the world didn't stack up too well against a lack of formal skills.

'As far as qualifications go I believe life experience is more important than a piece of paper. I've always been a people person, and I'm confident I can handle leading tour groups competently.'

She didn't add, *If I can handle your weirdo interview I think anything Alaska tosses my way will be easy.*

To her relief, he closed her résumé and tossed it on the desk.

'Though the job sounds adventurous your main role is customer service. Is that going to be stimulating enough for you?'

The way he said 'stimulating' almost sounded X-rated. What was wrong with her? The sooner she got to Alaska, surrounded by all that ice, the better.

Suave Superman had undermined her confidence and lowered her defences quicker than she could rebuild them. And when the walls tumbled, her common sense usually got lost in a tidal wave of useless emotions, like trust and believing not every man was a lying, cheating hound.

Now her outrage at his strange interviewing techniques had fled, she needed to get out of here. For the longer he stared at her with those all-seeing, too-intense blue eyes, the more chance she'd fluff it and he'd realise exactly how ill-equipped and underprepared she was to tackle a job of this magnitude.

'I'm looking forward to everything about this job.'

The moment her life in Sydney had fallen apart, she'd made a decision.

She could've wallowed, gone berserk on retail therapy, maxing out Daddy's Platinum in petty revenge. Instead, after a day's private pity party holed up in her favourite day spa, she'd realised what she had to do.

Grow a spine. Cast off her rose-coloured glasses. And do what she should've done years earlier.

Follow her dream.

'You're aware we cater to a high-end market? Luxury tours all the way?'

She nodded, confident in that aspect of her job. She'd grown up in moneyed circles, had rubbed elbows with the world's elite, so relating to them in this forum would be the least challenging aspect of her new job.

'Callum gave me a full rundown on the company. I'm looking forward to the challenge.'

His silence was disconcerting, his gaze too inquiring, too sceptical, too potent.

Keeping her voice crisp and businesslike, she forced a smile. 'Thanks for the opportunity. I won't let you down.'

She stood and offered her hand. As his fingers curled around hers the shock of physical contact shot up her arm and zapped her in places she'd deliberately ignored since learning the truth about Julian.

'Welcome to the team. I look forward to liaising with you.'

Nodding, she whirled around and strode across the office, anxious to reach the door. Her mind had conjured up all sorts of intimate ways she could *liaise* with her delectable new boss.

'Drop by tomorrow. Cheri will have your travel arrangements and training schedule waiting. Good luck, Jade. Great meeting you.'

His words sounded genuine as he opened the door for her and she briefly wondered if she'd imagined the whole bizarre scenario.

'Thanks. See you in six months.'

Great, she had the job. Not so great, her new boss had tied her up in knots and she thought he was hot, despite her personal vow to ignore men for…oh, the next millennium or so.

Luckily, Alaska and Vancouver were poles apart. She'd be traipsing around glaciers while he stayed behind his desk a thousand miles away. Perfect.

Nothing like a good dose of hypothermia to cool hyperactive hormones.

CHAPTER TWO

As JADE left his office, Rhys leaned back, exhaled slowly and rubbed his right temple where the beginnings of a headache hovered.

He didn't get headaches. Discounting the woman who'd just left. She was a headache just waiting to happen, every prissy inch of her.

From the top of her designer suit that would fund his payroll for a month to the bottom of her exorbitantly expensive shoes, Jade Beacham was one big headache.

She might be a stunner, with those endless legs, big breasts, huge dark Bambi eyes and long hair the colour of double-shot espresso, but he'd known the instant he'd first seen her snooping around the office she'd be more trouble than she was worth.

She had rich, uptight, society princess stamped all over her.

The expensive clothes, the immaculate make-up, the cultured accent, all added up to one thing. He'd lost his mind in hiring her, favour to her hot-shot dad not withstanding.

He hated owing anyone so when Fred had *requested* a job for his precious little girl, he'd reluctantly agreed.

Didn't mean he had to like it.

The moment she'd strutted down the corridor as if she owned the place, totally at home casing the joint when she should've been waiting, he'd wanted to make her jump through hoops, wanted her off guard.

So he'd gone through that odd scenario: testing her, pushing her, expecting her to fling her hair over one shoulder, hitch her designer bag higher and stroll out of here back to her cushy life.

She'd surprised him: by sticking around, by putting up with his crap and, most of all, by appearing genuinely happy when he'd given her the job.

It begged the question: why would a wealthy society princess need a job? Why here? What had happened to her life in Sydney for her to end up thousands of miles away?

Shaking his head, he snatched up the phone, not caring about the time difference between here and Melbourne. He needed to talk to Callum. Now.

'Callum Cartwright.'

'Hey, bro, you still at the office?'

An ear-splitting squeal gave him his answer before Callum responded.

'Uh-uh, I'm home minding the twins. Starr's understudy for the lead in *Mamma Mia*, and it's opening night.'

'Good for her.'

He paused as a 'gimme now' filtered down the phone, the demand so like Callum when he'd been a child that he laughed. 'Is that my favourite niece, the gorgeous Miss Polly?'

'Little tyrant more like it.'

A loud crash swiftly followed by tears had him grinning more as Callum cursed and muttered, 'Give me a minute, I'll be right back.'

'No worries.'

While his brother attended to domestic duties, he flicked through Jade's résumé, her lack of skills taunting him.

Realistically, if he hadn't owed Fred—who'd set him up with a major cruise line to use Wild Thing for their tours when he'd first started the business—he would've continued interviewing other candidates. But he didn't have time with another tour starting shortly. So he'd hired her, towering heels, sassy suit and all.

That figure-hugging suit had been something else: fitted jacket, pencil skirt, clinging to curves that made his hands itch. If she looked that good in a suit, he wondered what she'd look like in his preferred outfit for women: skin-tight jeans, turtle-neck sweater and a wind-break?

He bet faded denim would fit her just fine, hugging that great butt he'd glimpsed as she'd left his office, and for a crazy moment he regretted he wouldn't be around to find out.

The way her eyes had blazed and her lips had pursed when he'd flirted he guessed a fiery passion for life pounded through her veins. And where there was fire, there was usually a raging inferno of hot woman just waiting for a soothing touch to douse the flames.

It had been far too long since he'd played with fire, with any woman, and he had a sudden insane wish to see if Jade wanted to set off some pyrotechnics with him.

'I'm back.' Callum huffed into the phone while silence momentarily reigned. 'I've set them up with crackers and juice in front of the TV. That should give me about five minutes' peace.'

'Don't know how you do it.'

And he didn't, considering they'd never had a good role model for a father. Frank Cartwright had ignored both of them, only having time for their eldest brother, Archie. And once Archie had died in a car accident, their recalcitrant father had closed off completely.

Even now, after the successes they'd made of their lives, Frank rarely acknowledged them, acting as if his younger sons didn't exist. Which made Rhys admire Callum and the job he was doing with the twins even more.

'It's hard work, tougher than any business deal, but I love it.'

He heard the genuine emotion in his brother's voice, the sense of achievement, and for a split second he envied him. Not that he'd ever settle down long enough to have a family. Uh-uh, he'd leave that to the people who wanted ties to one place, to one person, and that sure as hell wasn't him.

Being emotionally invested with anyone, even kids, was tantamount to handing over his heart and begging for it to be carved up. Too risky, too painful, too masochistic.

'So what's up?'

Rubbing the spot over his left breastbone that had flared to life for a startling second, he tossed Jade's résumé back on his desk.

'I interviewed Jade Beacham today.'

'She's great.'

'Hmm…'

His non-committal response guaranteed Callum would push further.

'You didn't like her?'

He liked her too much, that was the problem, and it had nothing to do with her role as tour guide for the company.

'It's not that. She just seems too green.'

'We all had to start somewhere.'

Fair call, considering he'd spent years travelling the world after he'd finished his degree, moving from job to job, place to place, not willing to stop for fear the past—and the memories of his dead brother—would catch up with him.

If it hadn't been for Callum helping him set up Wild Thing he'd still be wandering, chasing shadows.

'You know Fred Beacham called in a favour to have me hire her?'

'Yeah, but after the initial screening I knew she'd be a good candidate anyway.' Callum paused, cleared his throat. 'You hate owing anybody anything. Is that what this is about?'

Rhys bit back his instant rebuttal. Was that why hiring the rich princess irked? Because he'd owed Fred and had had his favour called in?

Ignoring the question, he fired one of his own. 'You move in the same circles as the Beachams. Do you know why Fred was so gung-ho about a job for Jade?'

'Beats me.'

Callum paused as a long squeal interrupted their conversation, his resigned sigh making him chuckle. 'Haven't seen Fred socially for ages, not since the terrible two were born.'

Rhys laughed. 'You'd take a stake to the heart for those kids and you know it.'

'Got me.' Callum's rueful chuckles petered out. 'You coming to visit soon? Like sometime in the next decade or so, before they get their driving licences?'

'Yeah, yeah, sure,' he said, despising himself for how easily the lie tripped off his tongue. He had no intention of meeting his niece and nephew any time soon. Seeing their beaming faces in the photos Callum constantly emailed was bad enough, their toothy grins and chubby cheeks and all-round happiness exacerbating the sense of loss he strove to ignore every day.

Callum wouldn't be put off for ever but, thankfully, he let his reticence slide this time. 'Look, why don't you give Jade a trial? See how she handles the job for a few months?'

A few short months if he had anything to say about it. He hadn't stipulated a time frame with Fred, just agreed to give his darling daughter a job. Wouldn't be his fault if he had to fire her for incompetence.

'That's what I had in mind.'

A loud, prolonged shout of 'da-a-a-a-d-d-dy' heralded the end of their phone call.

'I'll leave you to it, bro.'

'Thanks for the call.'

Callum hesitated, making him wonder what was really going on with his reserved older sibling.

'From our initial interview I got the feeling Jade really needs a break. So give her a fair go, okay?'

'Shall do. Catch you later.'

As he hung up he managed a wry grin. Looked as if Jade had added his brother to her growing fan club.

'Excuse me, Rhys. Do you have a minute?' Cheri stuck her head around the door.

His latest secretary was the best he'd ever had: punctual, reliable and efficient, qualities he valued in an employee. Particularly skilled at handling problems, she dealt with them swiftly and with minimal fuss, allowing him to concentrate on running the company. And she didn't bat her eyelashes at him or wear microminis and bend over his desk like the last bimbo he'd had the misfortune to hire.

'Sure. What's up?'

He hoped his latest employee would be half as competent as Cheri, though he wouldn't mind if Jade batted her eyelashes at him. Not one little bit. As for bending over his desk in a short skirt...

'We have a problem.'

He wrenched his attention out of the gutter. Cheri wasn't prone to exaggeration so he braced himself for the worst.

'Allan called. He has glandular fever and won't be doing the season this year. I called our two back-ups and both are unavailable. What do you want me to do?'

He swore softly. The wilderness safaris couldn't run with three people, especially when one of them was a novice.

'Thanks, Cheri, leave it with me.'

She exited quietly, casting a worried glance in his direction.

'Damn.'

He grabbed the nearest pen, twirling it between his fingers, a stupid habit he had for doing his best thinking.

Wild Thing was more than a business; it was his pride and joy. He'd developed it from scratch, starting as a park naturalist for various national parks all around the world before migrating to Canada and venturing into the beautiful wilds of Alaska. He'd nurtured the idea of forming his own tour company and with dedication, patience and countless hours of hard work—plus the steadying influence of Callum—he'd finally succeeded.

This season promised to be the best yet, with two more cruise lines signing up for the luxury tours his company was famous for, and there was no way he'd squelch on a business deal.

The pen twirled faster the harder he thought, mulling over solutions as he stared at the print hanging on the opposite wall: a majestic bald eagle soared above snow-capped mountains, the caption FREEDOM in bold letters under it.

A germ of an idea sprouted in the back of his mind, yet he stifled it.

Don't even think about it.

However, the harder he tried to ignore it, the more it nagged until he couldn't focus on anything else.

Cursing under his breath, he picked up the phone. 'Cheri, tag me onto the travel arrangements you're making for Jade and the boys, and arrange my equipment. I'm going to Alaska.'

He slammed the phone down without waiting for a response and redialled before he had a chance to renege on the stupidest thing he'd done in a long while.

'Aldo, I need you in my office pronto. You're acting CEO for the next six months and we've a lot of planning to do. See you in five minutes.'

As he hung up on his deputy, he glanced at the print again. It mocked him. He hadn't felt free in a long time; responsibility and guilt put paid to that.

Now, he was heading back to the one place he truly loved and it scared him to death.

CHAPTER THREE

FOR the first time in her life, Jade had a job. A real, honest-to-goodness job, with a wage and co-workers and a boss who'd given her two sleepless nights in a row.

While acing the interview had been the confidence boost she needed, she still hadn't quite got her head around the interview itself.

Rhys Cartwright might be hot stuff, but the guy was seriously weird. All that subterfuge and play-acting reminded her of the people she'd left behind, though her parents and Julian would eclipse Rhys in the Oscar-winning stakes.

Shaking her head to dislodge the painful memories, she zipped her backpack shut and hoisted it onto her shoulders, wriggling to get comfortable, testing the weight.

Not bad, considering she'd over-packed as usual. She'd happily walked away from her couture ball gowns, had the foresight to pack all her winter gear. She'd probably stand out like a designer snowman in her gear but who cared? Didn't matter, as long as she did a great job and gained the reference she needed to enter uni as a mature biology student.

Pity weirdo boss with the Superman eyes wasn't coming to Alaska. He might be odd, but she could've really learned a lot from someone with his experience.

She'd done a Google search on him before the interview, had been blown away by his field experience. Rhys Cartwright wasn't your average CEO. He'd travelled the world after gaining his degree, had seen more places and done more exciting things than she'd ever dreamed about.

She envied him. While she'd been attending polo matches and nightclub openings and charity galas, he'd been out in the wilderness—the Amazon, the Arctic—making a difference.

Not that she hadn't loved her old life. She had, with every breath she took. But it had been a lie, all of it, and when the world as she knew it had collapsed around her ears she'd been left with the bitter knowledge the life she'd loved had been rather empty anyway.

She might have walked away from a brilliant marriage in the making and parents she'd idolised but, in shrugging off the constraints of her old life, she'd been reborn. Emotionally, psychologically, maybe even physically; for there was no other explanation for her irrational reaction to Rhys' raw sexuality.

Her hormones, bruised and battered from Julian's neglect while he'd focused on work, had jump-started in a big way the instant she'd met her charismatic boss. She should be relieved he wouldn't be accompanying her to Alaska.

Then why the annoying sliver of disappointment?

With an exasperated huff she dumped her backpack, rolled her shoulders and glanced at her watch. She had two hours before meeting her new co-workers at the airport. Back in Sydney, she would've grabbed a latte, surfed the Net on her iPhone or colour co-ordinated her outfit for that night's upcoming party.

Here in Vancouver, about to embark on the adventure of a lifetime, she did the only sane thing: flipped open her Lonely Planet guide and started reading.

Suck it up. You can do this.

Pasting a fake smile on her face—a smile honed through many years of attending gala functions as part of the Beacham brigade—Jade strode towards two men wearing Wild Thing polo shirts.

Her legs wobbled the entire journey across the tarmac as she wished for an errant plane to drop on her head.

Whatever made her think for one stupid second she could

swap stilettos for hiking boots, angora for anoraks? She was a novice, an inexperienced one at that, about to spend six months in the Alaskan wilderness.

Sure, she'd always loved nature, had thrived on school excursions to the Outback, to the Blue Mountains, her love of cold weather flourishing when her class had camped near the foot of Mount Kosciusko.

She'd begged her parents to take her camping after that. Predictably, they'd turned up their noses and chosen a first-class trip to a six-star spa resort in Thailand instead.

So she'd become smarter then, researching her favourite cold spots around the world—Val d'Isère in France, Queenstown in New Zealand, Sahoro in Japan—and pointing out the luxury accommodation and spa treatments to ensure her parents would visit. While they'd sunk cocktails in the bar and been smothered in caviar facials, she'd explored on her own, following trails off the beaten track, collecting local flora, revelling in the sub-zero temperatures.

She'd loved every second of those trips and now she had a chance to follow a secret passion: a true love of the outdoors. No way would she allow a last-minute attack of nerves to stop her.

Reaching the guys, she smiled and held out her hand.

'Jade Beacham.'

The taller guy shook her hand firmly. 'Pleased to meet you. I'm Jack Summer and this oaf is Cody Winter.'

Cody, shorter, rounder and shaggier—he reminded her of a giant teddy—elbowed his colleague and sent her a warm grin. 'Don't mind him. He lives in the wild most of the time.'

She laughed. 'Summer and Winter?'

The guys chortled. 'Strange, but true. Gets a laugh out of the tourists.'

'I bet.'

Jack cupped his ear. 'Is that an Aussie accent I hear? You from Down Under?'

'Sydney.'

She loved the buzz of the Harbour city: the vibe, the excitement, the eclectic mix of people and restaurants and shops.

Sydney never slept, the perfect party town for a party princess. Who had flung off her crown, kicked off her glass slippers and left her Prince Charming to turn back into the toad he was.

'Did you go to the Olympics? That would've been awesome!'

She shook her head, remembering the prissy party she'd attended with her folks instead. She'd been mad keen to attend the opening ceremony, but her folks had been invited to Dubai for the launch of some new hotel so they'd flown there, followed by a whirlwind visit to London and a stopover in Paris for a soirée on the way home.

She'd missed the whole Olympics but in typical Beacham fashion, Daddy had taken her to the next Olympics in Athens, flying first-class all the way.

'No, I missed out. Watched it on TV though.'

She could see Cody, the more perceptive of the two, noted her discomfort.

'Don't worry, Aussie girl. Where we're going you'll see more sport than you could ever wish for.'

'Really?'

The image of fierce lumberjacks in checked jackets sprang to mind though, apart from fishing, she didn't think Alaska had much sport.

Jack rolled his eyes. 'You ain't seen nothing 'til you've seen the way the tourists pour off the cruise ships, trample through the bush, jostle each other for the best position in the bus or canoe, then push and shove their way towards the food at the end of a tour. A medal-winning performance to the last person standing.'

She laughed, relieved the boys had a sense of humour. It would make the next six months a lot easier if they didn't resent the newbie and concentrated on making her laugh instead.

'Hey, boss, come to wish us bon voyage?'

Jack's question came from left field as a strange prickling awareness raised the hairs on the nape of her neck.

Someone stood close behind her. Too close. She didn't need

to turn to know who it was: her flip-flopping belly was a great recognition device.

'No bon voyage. This time I'm coming along to keep an eye on you.'

Oh, no...

Not wanting to appear rude, she turned, sent him a curt nod in greeting.

Rhys Cartwright had lost the suit; unfortunately, faded denim jeans highlighted lean legs, the bottle-green polo shirt increasing the impressive breadth of his shoulders. Yep, definitely a superhero bod. And now he was coming with them? No way.

'That's great, boss.' Cody extended a hand.

Yeah, real great.

'Cool.' Jack shook his hand too as she surreptitiously cleared her throat, trying to ease the sudden constriction at the thought of Rhys accompanying them.

While the boys busied themselves with the luggage and equipment, Rhys leaned closer, invading her personal space with his own special brand of ka-pow.

'Needless to say, I'll be watching you too.'

His ice-blue eyes pinned her with their brilliance as she suppressed a shudder of anticipation. Must be her eagerness to learn from him. Yeah, that was why her tummy tumbled and her palms grew clammy at the thought of spending six long months in the wilderness with her new boss. Her story and she was sticking to it.

'You don't have to worry. I'll do my best.'

And she fully intended to. She had no intention of botching this opportunity and ending up with her dreams in tatters. Or, worse, having to return to Sydney embarrassed.

'All very well and good, but is your best going to be good enough?'

His low voice might have been laced with amusement, but his wary stare hadn't eased. If anything, he was studying her with a strange intentness that raised goose bumps of foreboding.

It was almost as if he expected her to fail, as if he knew she had no real qualifications and had crammed that first-aid course over the last month to add to her CV so it wouldn't be a total blank.

She knew she could do this. She'd grown up around people from all walks of life, had socialised from the time she could talk, so how hard could it be leading a bunch of tourists around?

'You may be used to batting those long eyelashes to get what you want back home, Princess, but it isn't going to cut it where we're headed.'

Shock warred with indignation as she clamped her lips shut to stop her mouth from dropping open.

Princess? Implying she flirted her way through any situation? Where the hell did this guy get off?

As a host of indignant retorts pinged from her brain to her mouth, she caught the challenging gleam in his eyes, the smug expression.

He wanted her to bite back, wanted to rile her so she'd retaliate. Why? So he could fire her before she'd really started? Or was this more of the same warped game he'd started during that bizarre interview?

Whatever, she wasn't going to give him the satisfaction. She had a job to do, whether he wanted her here or not.

Mustering her best innocent expression, she gazed at him with fake demureness. 'Really? You don't think this will cut it in Alaska?'

She fluttered the very eyelashes he'd taken a swipe at, scoring a minor victory when his smile waned and he backed up a fraction.

So, he liked to be in control and didn't like to be challenged? She'd have to remember that if he gave her any more grief.

'If the eyelash thing doesn't work out, guess I could always use the *Princess* title, see how that impresses the plebs.'

Amusement gleamed in his piercing blue eyes, radiating a heat that curled her toes. 'For someone with no qualifications, in her first job, you're impressively poised.'

She wished he'd stop staring at her like that. She'd have no problem keeping warm in Alaska with those baby blues doing their thing.

Feigning nonchalance, she shrugged. 'I've handled bigger challenges.'

Like confronting her dad with what she'd seen, going to her mum with the truth, discovering her fiancé wasn't the guy she thought he was, escaping her old life because it was all one big sham and flying halfway around the world for a new start.

So, yeah, she knew a thing or two about challenges.

'Come on, you two. Get a move on. We've got a plane to catch.' Jack jerked his thumb towards a trolley where Cody was loading equipment.

Rhys turned away, but not before she'd seen the speculative expression on his face, as if he hadn't expected her to be so feisty. What did he expect? She might be inexperienced careerwise, but she'd handled a lot worse than him during her time on the Sydney party circuit.

Let him dish it out. She could take it.

Rhys chose that moment to bend and pick up his backpack, the faded denim clinging to his great butt, and her confidence evaporated as quickly as a glacier under the summer sun.

Professionally, she could handle anything.

Physically, her body was letting her down in a big way.

As he straightened and hoisted his pack onto his back she quickly snapped out of the butt-induced trance and gathered her bags. She had a large backpack and a small duffle bag, a far cry from the Gucci luggage her parents had given her for her six-month trip to Europe, a twenty-first birthday present six years ago. Thankfully, she'd stored it with the rest of her belongings back home, along with her bitter memories.

'Need a hand?'

His smile kick-started her heart all over again when she'd just steadied it into some semblance of normality after those blistering stares.

'Thanks, but I'm fine.'

'Suit yourself.'

She waited until he moved out of earshot before muttering, 'Princess, my butt.'

His mini-stumble would've gone unobserved but for the quick

grin he threw over his shoulder before he strode towards the plane without a backward glance while she lagged behind, lugging her bags, torn between ogling his tempting butt and wanting to plant her foot firmly in the middle of it.

'Don't straggle.' She heard the amusement in his taunt, the assured confidence he'd won this round.

No competition. Giving him a swift kick in the butt won hands down if she was silly enough to get that close.

CHAPTER FOUR

JADE had sipped Cosmopolitans at New York's trendiest bars, she'd savoured margaritas at exclusive Mexican Riviera resorts, she'd sculled flavoured vodkas in London's finest clubs, but nothing came close to the atmosphere of this chic, cosy bar tucked away off Skagway's main street.

A steel-and-glass enclosed fireplace radiated a welcoming heat in one corner, trendy chrome tables and chairs circled the room and a stainless-steel bar ran from the entrance to the back.

Soft jazz filtered through high-tech speakers, muted music clips flashed across a wide, flat screen suspended over the bar and the exotic cocktails distributed to patrons had her wondering if she'd stepped into a time machine and been whizzed back to Sydney.

But one glance behind the bar dispelled that illusion.

Some incredibly talented architect had captured the real beauty of Skagway and brought it directly into the bar with a monstrous clear glass pane that ran the entire length of the bar, allowing patrons to enjoy the towering snow-capped mountains as a background to their upmarket drinks.

She'd never seen anything like it and the view of all that rugged splendour had her itching to start her job.

As if reading her mind, Rhys raised his boutique beer in her direction before taking a long slug, looking just as comfortable here as he had in his slick designer suit in Vancouver.

He unnerved her but here she sat, playing at being the model employee, when every passing second made her more aware of him as a man rather than just a boss.

When he'd first suggested they have a drink for some company bonding, she'd been hesitant. But she couldn't beg off when Jack and Cody had been gung-ho so she'd tagged along, more than a little alarmed when the guys had ditched them after one beer in favour of one of the rowdier pubs they'd passed.

She'd been tempted to bolt too until she'd seen the gleam of challenge in Rhys's too-blue eyes. He'd expected her to do a runner too so she did the exact opposite, plonking her butt on a chair, ordering a soda and steeling her nerve for some meaningless small talk before she could make her escape.

'What do you think so far?'

Taking a sip of soda to ease the dryness in her throat the longer he stared at her, unwavering, as if he really valued her answer, she carefully replaced the glass on the table, annoyed when her hand trembled slightly. 'It's great. I can't believe I'm actually in Alaska.'

He chuckled, the laugh lines crinkling adorably around his eyes. 'You've only seen the airport and the main street so far. Are you really that impressed?'

She recalled the deep fjords they'd flown over and her first glimpse of the quaint Alaskan town that looked as if it hadn't changed in a hundred years.

'I love what I've seen. Can't wait to explore.'

He leaned across the table, creating an intimacy she found intoxicating yet terrifying.

'Lucky you've got such an experienced guide.'

'You really that good?'

His mouth quirked in a cocky smile that had her heart tripping and her head wishing she'd ordered something stronger than a soda.

'I'm better than good. I'm the best.'

She tried to ignore her pounding pulse, to focus on his lips as he spoke. Unfortunately, looking at his lips didn't help her concentration.

'That's a big call, Ranger. Sure you can live up to it?'

'You'll just have to try me and find out. You strike me as a girl looking for adventure and I think I've got just the thing for you.'

His eyes glimmered in the low light from a flickering votive candle in the middle of the table, conveying an enthralling danger that thrilled yet scared her.

Consuming heat swept through her body, burning everything in its path, including her common sense. She'd had a close call with a rat fiancé, had had her trust in the parents she loved shattered, yet here she was hanging on this guy's every flirtatious word. And not just any guy, he was her *boss*. Even if her common sense had gone AWOL she knew boss should equal hands off. *Should* being the operative word.

'And what would that be?'

'Six months in the most spectacular, unspoilt wilderness you'll ever see with an expert park naturalist as your personal guide. What more could a girl ask for?'

Oh, she could think of plenty of things, but wisely kept her wayward thoughts to herself.

'Tell me more.'

'What do you want to know?'

'Whether you fend off wild animals in your spare time?'

He laughed as she battled the instant image of Ranger Rhys shirtless, his torso glistening with sweat, muscles rippling as he wrestled a moose with his bare hands.

Perspiration peppered her brow at the thought as she surreptitiously dabbed it and gestured towards the fireplace. Yeah, as if *that* was making her hot.

'I enjoy the wilderness, if that's what you're asking.'

She wanted to ask more than that: such as how long he'd been here, how many tours he'd led, how many women he'd dazzled with those come-get-me eyes and wicked smile.

'Interesting. After seeing you at the office I figured you to be the businessman type. Relishing the head-honcho role, running the company from behind the comfort of your desk.'

His smile faded, shadows clouding those brilliant blue eyes to muted midnight.

'Yeah, guess I'm the typical suit now, though I don't see it as a bad thing.'

She noted the tensed shoulders, the sudden clenching of his fingers around the glass he held, and wondered who he was trying to convince.

'Grappling with figures can be just as rewarding as shooting the rapids. I haven't been out in the wild for two years and I don't miss it.'

His voice, devoid of all emotion, was a telltale sign in itself. His spiel sounded rehearsed, one he'd recited often by the sounds of it.

'You're kidding? Number crunching versus thrills and spills? If you're a park naturalist you must love the wilderness. Why haven't you been out in all that time?'

She could've bitten her tongue as his expression closed tight. He was her boss and she barely knew him. What on earth made her blurt out a question like that?

His body language screamed defensiveness, which meant he didn't want to talk about it. She knew better than this. She'd attended balls at international embassies all around the world, was usually the epitome of tact and diplomacy. Now, her social skills had deserted her, along with her self-confidence in reading people.

An awkward silence stretched as he stared into the bottom of his glass, his lips compressed and, though she should shut up, an unseen, previously undiscovered demon urged her to give it a last shot.

'Look, we're going to be colleagues for the next six months. Don't you think we should know a bit about each other, beyond the everyday niceties?'

His gaze lifted, the bleakness slamming into her, quickly replaced by the ferocity of one of the famed black bears she'd read so much about. So much for the meet-and-greet stage of their working relationship.

'If you're so keen on sharing secrets, why don't you tell me why you ran away from Australia and flew all the way out here, huh? And don't give me that bull about wanting to be a biologist because I don't buy it.'

Jade took a steadying breath. She'd started this, she'd have to finish it whether she liked it or not.

'I didn't run away. I needed a new start.'

Understatement of the year.

His stare bored through her as if he could read her mind. 'New start? Must involve a guy.'

'Why would you say that?'

She aimed for nonchalance, knowing it must look as if she'd swallowed a salmon whole.

'You're an intelligent, beautiful woman. Bet you had the guys lined up back in Sydney.'

A slow warmth suffused her cheeks at his compliment, the inner glow Julian had extinguished reigniting with the simple admiration from this man.

'Just one guy. He cheated on me.'

He winced. 'Sorry. What a jerk.'

She sighed, wishing she'd kept her mouth shut. She could tolerate probing questions; she couldn't stand his pity.

'All in the past now. Good incentive to focus on the future. No one to stand in my way now.'

'I admire your resolve.' He gestured to the barman, indicating another round. 'Same for you or would you like something stronger?'

'Soda's fine.'

So much for finding out more about him; once she'd flapped her loose lips, part of her pathetic life story had flowed out and the ship had well and truly sunk.

'I've told you my sorry tale—what's yours?'

He avoided her eyes, focusing on the table, the silence stretching like a taut highwire ready to snap.

'Come on, it can't be that bad,' she teased, trying to lighten the mood.

After the waiter cleared the glasses and replaced their drinks, Rhys looked up and her heart twisted at the despondency in his eyes.

'One of my tour guides died on my last tour.'

He shook his head, hopelessness evident in the dejected slump of his broad shoulders.

'You okay?'

She laid a tentative hand on his forearm, wishing she could think of the right thing to say and coming up with *nada*.

He threw off her hand, sat back so abruptly his chair scraped across the floorboards.

'You asked for my story, you got it. Ready to go?'

What could she say? No, she wasn't ready, because she wanted to know more about the tragic death that turned a carefree charmer into a bristling bore in an instant? No, that she wanted to apologise for pushing him when she barely knew him?

Swallowing her regrets, she nodded and followed him out of the door.

So much for shared confidences resulting in a better working relationship. The way he'd just glared at her, the glaciers wouldn't be the only things frozen over the next six months.

Nice going. Great ice-breaker technique.

Shaking her head in disgust, she wondered how to make up for her gaff.

CHAPTER FIVE

As THEY stepped out into the crisp night air, Jade took a few head-clearing breaths before falling into step beside Rhys, almost having to run to keep up with his long, angry strides.

Why the heck had she hounded him? She'd wanted to foster a good working relationship, not alienate him completely on her first day!

With his head bent, hands thrust into his jacket pockets, shoulders hunched against the howling wind, she had some serious work to do to resume the tentative working relationship she'd established earlier in the night.

'Hey.'

He glanced at her, his expression hidden in shadows. 'Leave it alone, Jade.'

She could leave it alone. She *should* leave it alone. But where would that leave them tomorrow? And the next day? And for the next six months when she tried to nail this job?

'Let's head back to the hotel.' He instantly picked up the pace, leaving her no option but to pull up the collar of her Gore-Tex parka and do the same rather than trail behind like a trained husky.

'Slow down.'

She doubted he heard, with the wind whipping her words away as soon as they left her mouth, and he continued stalking, huge strides that had her practically jogging along next to him.

Okay, so she'd pried into his personal business, opened an old wound that explained why he'd been stuck behind a desk the last two years, but if she didn't clear the air the next few months could be tough.

'Hold up.'

She reached out, tugged at his jacket, startled when he stopped abruptly and she slammed into his back.

'Ouch!'

She rebounded and would've fallen if he hadn't grabbed her, imprisoning her in a vice grip.

'What now?'

She could barely see in the dim street lighting, but heard the exasperation in his voice.

'We need to talk about this.'

'No, we don't.'

He hadn't eased up with the Tarzan grip and her concern quickly morphed into something else, something a lot like a woman all too aware of six feet plus of hot, sexy male within touching distance.

'You're ticked off. Not a good start to our working relationship. I don't want to leave things like that.'

She bit down on her tongue, realising she was babbling and wishing she could tuck her Gore-Tex between her legs and high-tail it back to the hotel like a good little employee, leaving her Pinocchio nose out of his business.

'Like what?'

'Tense. Awkward.'

She shrugged, feeling more foolish by the minute, a feeling that only increased as she focused on the patch of smooth bronze skin at the base of his throat where his parka zip didn't go all the way up.

The colour of his skin matched her favourite crème caramel dessert, oh, so tempting A bizarre urge to lick it popped into her mind as an inane craving to taste him urged her to close the short gap between them and… Just one little lick, surely that wouldn't be harmful? Yeah, just as the calories never went straight to her hips when she ate the real thing.

Lost in a fanciful haze, she missed the moment he loosened his grip and started running his hands over her upper arms, and though she wore a woollen jumper under the parka her skin tingled.

'Doesn't seem too tense now.'

She stared at his lips, transfixed. The last thing she needed was a kiss from her boss. What she wanted, now that was a different matter entirely.

Her eyelids fluttered shut and she tilted her head up, eager to feel that first liberating explosion of sensation when lips fused.

No kiss was as electrifyingly exciting as a first kiss and she had a feeling Rhys would know all the right moves. He had the attitude, the confidence, the lips that just begged to be kissed and she'd forgotten every sane reason why she shouldn't.

She waited, every second an exquisite lesson in torturous anticipation, every second taunting her with a million logical arguments why she should pull away now and make a run for it.

'Damn it!' He muttered a string of soft curses under his breath as he released her, the air between them suddenly frigid as her eyes flew open to be confronted by a broad expanse of back.

He'd been a sigh away from their lips touching and he'd had the willpower to stop the kiss. Willpower *she* should've had.

Mortified, she didn't know whether to laugh it off or pretend it hadn't happened. Yeah, as if that were an option.

She knew it was for the best he hadn't kissed her their first night in Alaska; mixing business with pleasure was crazy, especially when she'd have to spend the next six months with him. Then why did she want to blubber like a jilted wallflower on prom night?

'Well, I guess we're back to tense again.'

Her false laugh grated, but they had to get past this, had to forge some kind of working relationship. No way was she heading back to Australia without some decent work experience on her CV to help facilitate her entry into university.

He turned, his gaze raking over her yet giving away little as he ruffled the dark hair curling slightly over his collar.

'Won't be tense if we forget that ever happened.'

His calm voice and confident stance were at complete odds

with her tumbling belly and quivering resolve. She should've admired him for it; instead, his cool nonchalance aggravated her beyond belief.

Of course they should forget it. But ignoring the four-hundred-pound bear in the corner of the igloo wouldn't make it go away, and no way could she survive the next six months with this tension humming between them.

'So we're supposed to forget the fact you almost kissed me?'

His lips curved into the kind of smile that made forgetting the urge to kiss him impossible.

'Maybe you almost kissed me?'

'No way! *You* were holding me, *you* leaned towards me, *you*—'

'I get the picture.'

He shook his head, but his smile merely widened. 'Must've lost my head for a moment. Forgive me?'

With that cheeky smile and naughty gleam in those incredible blue eyes, how could she refuse?

Besides, nothing to forgive. She'd wanted that kiss so badly she'd practically invited it: leaning into him, tilting her head, closing her eyes...

She inwardly cringed, outwardly fixing the serene expression she'd used to great effect at many a boring function.

'Forgotten.' She snapped her fingers. 'Just like that.'

'Good.'

She should've been relieved they'd brushed over it so easily, should've been grateful they could laugh at it thanks to his handling of the situation.

But there was nothing remotely like relief or gratitude simmering between them as they stood there, gazes locked, the frosty air steaming from the short breaths they exhaled, the tension buzzing between them as potent as ever.

She had to escape before she did something foolish—again.

'I'm heading back to the hotel. See you in the morning.'

He nodded. 'I won't be far behind you. 'Night.'

As she picked her way along the pavement, more carefully this time, she felt his stare burning into her back and it took every ounce of her meagre willpower not to look back.

Rhys kept Jade in his sight as he followed her.

He'd acted like a jerk at the end of their drinks session in the bar, an even bigger jerk for almost kissing her as a distraction technique.

She'd got too damn close in the bar, her doe-eyed stare all soft and encouraging, and he'd nearly blurted out the truth of why being back here stung.

It had been a close call and he couldn't afford to let the princess playing pauper creep under his guard.

At least he'd learned her reason for being here. It had less to do with her urge to study biology and more to do with some idiot who'd cheated on her.

She was running away from her old life, dabbling for a while, before she'd head back to her gowns and baubles.

It should annoy him, the fact she was using a job most people would give their eye teeth for as an escape, but he understood. Boy, did he understand the driving need to run when the going got tough.

As for that kiss… His initial plan to shock her into forgetting the awkwardness following his blurted admission had vanished the moment he'd touched her.

It had been an impulse, something guaranteed to shock her. Ironic, he'd been the one shocked with how close he'd come to losing control when she'd stared at him with those big brown eyes, her sensual mouth an inch away…

For that split second between going through with a callous kiss that meant nothing, a calculated kiss meant to distract, and sensibly pulling back, he'd ached to hold her, to touch her, to bury his face in her sleek chocolate-brown hair.

Thankfully, he hadn't gone through with it and she'd handled his idiocy with aplomb, demonstrating what he already knew. Jade Beacham had class and then some.

He'd moved in the same social circles many moons ago, had met girls like her as a teenager. Pampered, pretty princesses with high expectations and endless credit via Daddy's gold card. If it sounded like a princess and acted like a princess, it expected to be treated like one.

He'd escaped early enough to never get involved with one and had determinedly avoided that type of woman since. Playing lackey to a high-maintenance woman just wasn't his style.

Uh-uh, when he'd finally opened his heart to a woman, it had been someone the absolute antithesis of a pampered princess.

And look what had happened as a result.

Cursing soundly, he headed towards the hotel. This wasn't the time for another lapse in judgement. It was hard enough just being back in this town.

With Jade's curvy image imprinted on his brain, and the answering spark he'd glimpsed in her beautiful brown eyes, he had a feeling things were about to get a lot harder.

CHAPTER SIX

JADE rolled out of bed and stumbled to the bathroom as the pale dawn light filtered through the curtains. She glanced in the mirror, not surprised to see dark rings under her eyes. After a sleepless night, what did she expect?

Stepping under the shower, she tilted her head back, allowing the warm water to sluice over her face. She shampooed her hair, soaped her body and shaved her legs, focusing on the mundane tasks in a futile attempt to block out the memory of last night— and the cringe-worthy fact she'd almost kissed her boss.

She'd lain awake half the night replaying every tension-fraught moment since she'd met Rhys Cartwright. After that bizarre interview and her original initiation into the company, she should've known things would go downhill.

Though for a brief moment in the bar last night, she'd felt a connection, a genuine sharing of information that led to bonding.

Before she'd botched it all big time and made a mess of everything.

She'd lied to him. She'd told him the kiss was forgotten when in reality it was all she could think about. She couldn't forget the feel of his strong hands stroking her arms, his intoxicating outdoorsy-woody smell, those blue eyes heavy with passion, the sight of his lips descending towards hers...

With one last icy blast she turned off the taps and stepped out of the shower. The rush of cold air raised goose bumps over her damp skin; or was her physiological reaction a result of imagining Rhys's kiss?

Her hands shook as she dried off, the nerves she'd managed to subdue in the shower taking flight again. How on earth was she going to face him today?

No matter how efficiently they'd brushed it off last night, pretended it never happened, she'd have to show up to her first day on the job all perky and bouncy and enthusiastic when inside she'd be a quivering mess.

Shrugging into her robe, her gaze landed on her toiletry bag propped on the bathroom counter.

There lay her answer.

Whenever she'd had to attend a big event in the past, whether afternoon tea with royalty or polo with a prince, she'd ensure she looked her best. Perfect make-up, styled hair, killer outfit. Looking good gave her confidence and if ever there was a time she needed a boost, this was it.

She donned stretch black pants, a sapphire jumper and the latest design in hiking boots, then concentrated on the onerous task of applying make-up. Keeping the colours neutral, she applied a light foundation and translucent powder, outlined her eyes with blue kohl, smudged a bronzed eyeshadow over her lids, whisked the mascara wand over her eyelashes and finished off with a smidgeon of pale pink lip gloss.

Not bad. The make-up provided an excellent confidence mask, though it was difficult to disguise the doubt in her eyes. Her windows to the soul definitely needed some new blinds.

She snacked on a bagel to quell her rolling tummy as she quickly repacked and ten minutes later joined the guys down at the wharf awaiting their JetCat transport. After handing over her backpack to the transport staff, she took a deep breath and headed down the wooden planks.

A long, low wolf whistle heralded her arrival. 'Look at you.' Jack gave her a thumbs up, his grin appreciative.

'Wow.' Cody winked, staring at her over the top of his sunglasses and wriggling his eyebrows suggestively.

She smiled at the guys, her confidence slipping when Rhys turned, his eyes inscrutable behind mirrored shades.

'A bit much for where we're going, though the grizzlies may be impressed,' he said, before turning his back and squatting to fiddle with the straps on his pack.

Jade's smile didn't slip despite her utter deflation at his comment. Not that she'd been expecting a compliment. She'd done all this for herself, right?

'Are you blind? We've got a stunner in our midst and you think it's a bit much? You've spent too much time behind your desk. Your brain is oxygen-starved.' Jack glared at Rhys's back before poking out his tongue.

'I second that. You're becoming a fuddy-duddy, boss. Time to get you back out there so you can live a little,' Cody said, grinning. 'After all, if you can't appreciate a beautiful woman you must be blind, half-dead, or both.'

Jade resisted the urge to high-five the boys as Rhys's shoulders stiffened, but he didn't respond.

'Don't worry about him. He's been like a bear with a sore head all morning.' Jack dropped his voice low and jerked his thumb towards Rhys. 'Probably just nerves about being out in the field again. Been a long time between drinks for our fearless leader. We think he's as twitchy as a bull in mating season.'

Cody groaned and grabbed Jack by the arm. 'You're talking to a lady, remember?'

Jack shuffled his feet, eyes downcast. 'Sorry, Jade.'

She loved seeing the two friends interact; it was like watching a comedy skit. 'Don't worry about it. I'm just one of the boys for the next six months.'

'Is that so?'

She turned, unaware Rhys had snuck up behind her.

'We'll continue checking the packs,' Cody mumbled, both men ambling away while pulling faces behind Rhys's back.

She tilted her head up, wishing he weren't so darn tall. Hard to be forthright and intimidating when he towered over her.

'I don't want any special favours. I'm more than capable of doing my fair share and I want the guys to feel comfortable around me, not having to watch their p's and q's every second I'm around.'

'Do you really think it'll be that easy?'

The speculative gleam in his eyes didn't inspire confidence. In fact, she deflated quicker than a rubber dinghy punctured with a pine needle.

She thrust her chin up, determined not to show him how much he rattled her.

'Only one way to find out, isn't there, *boss*? You're stuck with me, for better or worse.'

His mouth twitched at her sass. Definitely only one way to handle this guy: give as good as she got.

'I prefer Rhys from you,' he said, his voice low, intimate, sending a shiver skittering through her hyper-aware body.

'Don't like to think of me as an employee, huh?'

His eyes darkened to indigo, the latent heat between them sparking in an instant as she instantly regretted her urge to bait him.

Forgetting that almost-kiss was one thing, sparring with him another. For that was exactly what she was doing: fencing with him using words, parrying his quips, enjoying the comebacks.

She'd always been a sucker for a quick brain. It had been one of the things that had attracted her to Julian in the first place. Pity the orthopaedic surgeon's intelligence didn't extend to common sense and common decency.

'Honestly? I have no idea how to think of you.'

With a shake of his head, he broke the spell binding them. 'You're confusing the hell out of me.'

With a funny half-salute, he walked away, leaving her just as confused.

After a forty-minute ride on the JetCat, one of the fastest passenger catamarans in North America, they were offloaded on a black, pebble-lined shore at Glacier Point.

Jade turned a slow three hundred and sixty, absorbing the impact of the unspoilt beauty. Majestic, snow-capped mountains surrounded them, distant waterfalls glittering as they tumbled to meet the deep fjords below. Forest-green pines silhouetted sharply against a cloudless sky the colour of…Rhys's amazing blue eyes.

With a mental shake, she inhaled, savouring the pure air, the damp earthy smell a reminder of school camps in the Blue Mountains. The bulk of her classmates from the exclusive girls' school she'd attended had preferred to sit in their cabins and give each other manicures while she'd snuck off, clutching her secret love of nature close, revelling in the untamed bush, the crisp mountain air, the bite of breaking dawn.

Later, when her buddies at finishing school were jetting off to Monte Carlo and Cancun and Morocco for their holidays, she'd head for the nearest ski fields, eager to be near her beloved mountains again, keen to savour the invigorating splendour of snow.

She glanced at Rhys, who'd barely spoken for the entire journey. He also appeared mesmerised, though a fleeting anguish crossed his face as he focused on the endless cerulean water.

She hadn't pushed him for information about who'd died on his last tour, hadn't wanted to pry despite her burning curiosity, but seeing his visible reaction to this place piqued her interest.

What made a guy like him tick?

Was he best suited to his desk, wheeling and dealing as the company CEO, or was the laid-back park naturalist she'd glimpsed over drinks last night the real Rhys Cartwright?

'Come on, guys, let's get this show on the road. Time to load up and ship out.' Rhys deliberately glanced her way. 'That includes you too, Princess. From now on when I say guys, you're included, just like you wanted.'

'Fine by me.'

She hadn't called him on the Princess nickname yet. He wanted her to; she could see it in the blatant challenge in his eyes, exactly why she wouldn't bite.

The corners of his lips curved into a smug smile as he turned away, giving her prime view of dark denim moulding his butt and the cream cable-knit sweater hugging the muscular contours of his back.

He was so *hot*, and she wondered for the hundredth time since she'd scored this job what had happened to her physically. She'd never been this turned on around Julian, even though she'd found the sex fun; when they'd had it. Julian had been tired, often, and she'd accepted it as part of being a doctor's fiancée. Sadly, she'd discovered the true reason for his fatigue; shagging two women at once must be hell on a guy's endurance.

'Earth calling Jade. Did you hear me?'

She wiped the scowl threatening to crease her face, her gaze wandering from his chest to his eyes.

'Sorry, momentarily distracted by the awesome ruggedness of all of this.'

She almost bit her tongue in frustration. That sounded so lame. Thinking about Julian had shattered her cool; though perving at Rhys had already ensured meltdown.

He grinned. 'Thanks.'

'For what?'

'The compliment.'

She rolled her eyes. 'I was talking about the scenery.'

'Really?'

His loaded stare told her he didn't buy her excuse for a second and she flushed, grateful he'd turned away before she could wipe that cocky grin off his face.

With what? Her witty comebacks?

With a resigned huff, she picked up her backpack and shrugged into it.

First the almost-kiss, now this. If he'd had any doubts before he'd now know for certain she thought he was the hottest guy she'd seen in ages. Sheesh, she'd practically drooled watching him bend over.

Rhys Cartwright had brains as well as brawn and she'd need to keep that in mind. Either that or search for the biggest lump of kryptonite she could find. Wasn't that the only thing that would keep Superman at bay?

'Okay, let's go. Accommodation's around the next bend.'

Excitement fizzed through her veins like the finest champagne as she fell into step beside Rhys, content to absorb the beauty of her surroundings, the companionable silence a change from his flirting or her lame comebacks.

Not that she minded the flirting. She just wished she knew how to handle it better. Was he doing it because she was the only female around or did he genuinely fancy her?

As her foot caught on a tree root and she stumbled she knew she'd be better off focusing on her job than her boss.

'You okay?'

'Fine, just clumsy,' she said, keeping her gaze fixed on the well-worn path through the bush, her attention captured by the staggering array of plant and flower species.

'You're really into this stuff.'

She heard the surprise in his voice, risked a glance his way, the respect in his penetrating stare making her want to skip through the bush.

'You think I want to head back to uni as a mature student for the fun of it?'

He had the grace to look uncomfortable. 'Not many people would be doing this.'

'What? This?'

She reached out, touched a delicate leaf with tenderness, fingering the softness, capturing a dew drop on her fingertip.

'I love nature.'

'But?'

'But the closest I've come in a while is Taronga Zoo.'

'Sheltered upbringing?'

'Different world, more like it.'

The dew drop dripped off her fingertip, disappeared into the forest floor cover and she swallowed, dismayed to discover talking about her past, even in general terms, was enough to bring a lump to her throat.

'Well, being here is going to get you where you want to go so come on, let's get you settled.'

He hadn't pushed her. On the contrary, he'd sensed her discomfort, and had diverted attention from it.

She didn't know what was worse: Rhys at his teasing best or

this intuitive, kind Rhys. Both had the potential to undo her in a second.

'Are we staying in cabins?'

His earlier compassion faded, replaced by something she'd almost describe as fear. That couldn't be right. Sure, he'd mentioned the death of someone on his last tour, but had it affected him to the extent he was scared of being back here?

Somehow, she couldn't see big, bold Rhys Cartwright afraid of anything.

'We're staying in the house.'

'The house?'

She didn't have time to probe further as they rounded a bend and Rhys pointed dead ahead.

'Home, sweet home.'

Jade stopped dead, her mouth hanging open like some sideshow clown.

'*House*? This place is…'

She shook her head, blinked, and refocused on a picture-perfect advertisement taken straight from Discovery Channel's Top Ten luxury homes around the world.

'You like?'

The catch of vulnerability underlying his tone surprised her as much as his expectant expression. He wanted her to like it, wanted her approval. For whatever reason, she couldn't fathom why. Instead, she smiled.

'It's the most gorgeous *house* I've ever seen. And I use the term house loosely.'

Instantly entranced by the sandstone mansion silhouetted against the snow-capped mountains, she marvelled at its architecture: the different levels, the various wings appearing to spread across the hillside, blending into the landscape perfectly, at one with nature.

The mansion sprawled across half an acre, its large glass windows reflecting the morning sun, giving it a welcome appeal rather than looking like a mausoleum as so many mansions she'd visited in the past could appear.

'I built it.'

Her eyebrows shot up as she glanced at the man who never stopped surprising her.

He smiled. 'Not literally. I had a major hand in the design, wanted it to fit into the landscape and not detract from all this.'

He threw his arms wide, encompassing their surroundings, his spontaneous gesture and concern for the environment attracting her as much as the rest of him.

'It's gorgeous.'

'Sure is.'

He stared directly at her in a blatant declaration he wasn't just talking about the scenery. His burning gaze travelled the length of her body, a slow, leisurely perusal that left her breathless as she imagined his fingertips following the same path, setting her whole body alight.

She dragged in a breath, finding the simple process of breathing difficult. The slight movement of parting her lips drew his eyes like magnets as he stared at her glossed lips for what seemed like an eternity, flicking the tip of his tongue out to moisten his own.

And at that very moment she'd never wanted to kiss a man as much.

She could blame the fresh air; maybe her brain only functioned on city pollution, not purity. But she'd be lying, and if there was one thing she'd learned from the fiasco with her parents and Julian, it was never to lie. To anybody, particularly herself.

'Time to get settled,' she murmured, reluctant to break the tenuous link binding them yet wanting to snap it faster than she could say 'iceberg'.

He nodded, the sensual cocoon just for two evaporating in an instant.

'You take the east wing, the boys are in the west.'

'And I suppose you'll have the run of the place, being the lord of the manor.'

She'd meant it as a joke. By the lack of laugh lines and his rigid posture, he found it far from funny.

'If you follow the path to your right, you'll find a side door.

Should be open. The couple who housekeep when its empty expected us. Give a holler on the intercom if you need anything.'

Brisk, businesslike instructions, at complete odds with his loaded stare a few moments ago. She juggled her backpack into position, eager to get inside and out of the cold. Literally.

'Thanks, I'll be right there.'

With a brief nod, he headed for the main entrance, leaving her to ponder exactly how complex her boss was—and whether she could be bothered trying to understand more.

CHAPTER SEVEN

THE moment Rhys stepped through the front door his chest tightened, as if a giant grizzly had him in a bear hug and were squeezing the life out of him.

He couldn't breathe, the tightness expanding until he forced oxygen into his lungs by inhaling great gulps of air.

The place looked the same, as warm and cosy and inviting as the day he'd left.

He loved it, from the pale ash polished boards, soaring ceilings, cream walls and windows overlooking Glacier Point and beyond, to the steel-rimmed open fireplace, modular light fittings and thick Persian rugs.

It was his dream home. He'd never had a home growing up. Sure, he'd lived in the same house as his brothers and parents, but there'd been nothing homely about that scenario. His parents ignored him, Callum was too busy rebelling in a futile effort to capture their attention and Archie...well, Archie had been the only Cartwright to acknowledge he existed.

He'd idolised his eldest brother, had tried to emulate him: good grades, captain of the cricket team, lead cellist in the school orchestra.

Then Archie had died, a senseless waste of life, and his world had been tipped on its head.

Callum, riddled by misplaced guilt he'd caused Archie's death—after a late night call to pick him up from the local jail when a bunch of drunk kids had been taken in for yahoo-ing and Archie had been killed in a car crash on the way there—had stepped into Archie's big shoes, entering the family financial business at nineteen.

While his big brother had dealt with his grief by throwing himself into business, Rhys had coped the only way he knew how. By running away. And he hadn't stopped running since.

He didn't do commitment well. Getting attached to anyone or anything just wasn't worth the effort. He could've blamed his quest for freedom on his narcissistic parents or lack of desire for attachment on Archie's death, but it was more than that.

The only time he felt truly alive was when he was free. Free of entanglements, free of emotions, free of energy-sapping ties.

Swiping a weary hand across his face, he reopened his eyes, confronted by the beauty of the house, sucker-punched again.

When he'd originally built the house, he knew what he'd been doing. Trying something new, testing to see if he could emotionally invest in something, to see if he cared about something enough he could stay if he wanted to.

His experiment had failed spectacularly.

He'd lived here for two years until the urge had crept upon him again: the urge to cut ties, the urge to cut loose, the urge to move on to the next challenge.

And he'd done it. Walked away from this place without a backward glance and hadn't been back since.

Claudia's death precipitated his prolonged absence but in reality if his guilt over her death hadn't sent him running, this place and all it stood for—family, kids, roots, a place to call home, a resting place where he could finally find peace—would've eventually done the trick.

For that split second when he'd seen Jade's wondrous expression and her admiration for his dream, all the old yearnings had come flooding back in an unbearable wave. Worse, he'd pictured her standing right there next to him. Impossible, what with her life plan, even if he was stupid enough to contemplate getting emotionally involved for more than a second.

He didn't want to like her so much. But there was no denying the woman he'd pegged as a rich society princess slumming it for a while was a trouper.

She'd put up with his boorish behaviour this morning because he'd almost kissed her, she'd been nothing but enthusiastic and happy and eager to learn on the JetCat over here.

He needed to cut her some slack.

As his gaze drifted to the spectacular glacier shimmering in the distance he crossed to the window, braced his hands against the glass.

He needed to chill out and nothing centred him more than a visit to his favourite place on earth.

The east wing charmed Jade the moment she stepped through the door. If the outside of the house held her enthralled, the inside far surpassed her wildest dreams.

The *wing* was the size of an average suburban house, a huge open-plan room consisting of leather lounge suite with recliner chairs, a flat-screen TV the size of a bed sheet, state-of-the-art sound system and a sleigh bed that could fit a family of Santa's elves quite comfortably.

Throw in the honey-coloured floorboards and matching beams soaring overhead, the squishy rugs underfoot, the kitchenette and monster bathroom, and she could happily live here for the next six months.

But by far the most attractive feature of the room was the one-hundred-and-eighty-degree floor-to-ceiling windows overlooking a breathtaking vista. Towering snow-capped mountains, lush green forests and an incredible ice glacier that sparkled a pristine blue in the pale sunlight.

Crossing to the glass, she reached out, touched it, imagined touching the ice. A shiver of excitement shot through her. Being here felt good. And she hadn't felt good in a long time.

She didn't go in for spiritual stuff, but the moment she'd set foot on Glacier Point she'd been buzzing with the rightness of all this.

Her hand slipped down the glass, her fingertips the last lingering contact before she shook her head. Now wasn't the time for fanciful ideas. She had enough to do, starting with the many challenges of a new job and ending with keeping her hands off her new boss.

The glacier snagged her attention again and she couldn't look away. On the JetCat Rhys had told them they could have the morning off to settle in. Glancing across at her backpack, she wrinkled her nose. Plenty of time to unpack. Right now, she'd rather get out there and explore. Besides, a good dose of bracing fresh air might prepare her for the afternoon's orientation with the boss.

When they'd arrived at the house she'd sensed his tenseness, had heard the brittle undertone in his voice. Being back here affected him more than he let on and an uptight boss did not make for a stress-free introduction to working life.

Yep, she definitely had to calm herself before this afternoon and what better way than a few hours with her first up close and personal experience of a glacier?

Jade followed a worn, muddy path through the forest, stepping over rocks and exposed tree roots. Despite taking care she stumbled several times, the slippery surface underfoot as disconcerting as the thought of starting her new job.

She'd been running on adrenalin until now, muscling her way into that pre-screening back in Sydney, organising the logistics to make the interview in Vancouver, arriving determined to nail the job, feigning confidence since she'd learned the boss himself would be on this tour.

Now she'd actually arrived, the reality of her situation hit home.

She had absolutely zero experience in leading luxury wilderness tours, no customer service skills and a limited knowledge of the local area despite swotting up on every book and Internet site she could find.

Rhys expected the best. He'd said so during the interview. The interview she'd swanned through with loads of fake bravado and little hands-on experience.

She might desperately need this job to facilitate her entry into university, but now she'd arrived, completely overwhelmed by the beauty and vastness of the place, the reality of what she was letting herself in for hit home.

She needed to be the best darn tour guide Wild Thing had ever employed. Failure wasn't an option.

No pressure on you, then.

Wincing, she rounded a trailhead and entered a small clearing, gasping at the breathtaking glimpse of her first glacier up close.

Wow.

If seeing the glacier from the house had made an impact it was nothing compared to standing on a pebbled foreshore, wishing she could reach out and touch the sheer icy face.

She couldn't breathe; like the first time she'd laid eyes on her boss, actually.

As if her thoughts conjured him up, he stepped into view from behind a clump of trees and her lungs constricted, protesting the lack of oxygen as she observed him unnoticed.

Standing on a rocky outcrop surveying the scenery, he looked at one with nature. His profile, with those high-slashed cheekbones and cut-glass jaw, reminded her of the glacier's sharp angles: as impressive, as rugged, as beautiful.

Even from a distance she could sense his tension, his posture abnormally straight, his shoulders rigid. Definitely her cue to leave.

Easing backwards, she stepped on a twig, shattering the silence: His head snapped towards her in an instant, his expression shuttered.

She pasted a smile on her face while inwardly cursing her klutziness as he strode towards her, long legs encased in denim, legs used to going places and getting there damn fast.

'What do you think of my favourite spot?'

She stared at the majestic icy peak, the sun reflecting off its shimmering surface, sending shards of cool gentian into the horizon, opening her mouth to find the right words and failing, eventually settling for, 'It's unbelievable.'

His face relaxed into a smile. 'I had the same reaction first time I saw Davidson Glacier.'

They stood in silence, looking at the glacier, while she snuck glances at him, relieved he'd lost the brooding expression.

When he'd first spotted her, she'd half expected him to be angry at her for intruding on his turf, but thankfully he'd relaxed enough to tolerate her being here.

'Exploring?'

She nodded, all too aware of their seclusion now he stood a foot away. When she'd been alone, the magic of this place had amplified. But with him in her personal space—as big and daunting as the ancient pines surrounding them—the vastness had shrunk, leaving the two of them too close.

'Yeah, I saw the glacier from my window, was keen to take a closer look.'

'How close do you want to get?'

She swallowed, sure there was nothing remotely suggestive about his question, but her errant mind focused on that stupid almost-kiss again, reading too much into every little nuance, every little word.

'Uh—'

'See those canoes down there? They're not just for show.'

She blushed, tried to cover her embarrassment with pep. 'Lead the way, Ranger.'

He hadn't called her on the nickname and she wondered if he was as afraid of broaching it as she was. Nicknames implied intimacy, friendship, two things she should shy away from with him.

'Come on.'

They continued down the trail for another half mile before reaching the lake, where a huge canoe lay beached on the rocky sand.

'Your chariot, Princess?'

He picked up an oar and held it out to her like a prized glass slipper. Not that she believed in that particular fairy tale. She knew all too well how fast princes could turn into frogs.

'What's with the Princess tag?'

'A term of endearment.' He grinned, a carefree smile that held tones of the cheeky boy he must've once been. 'Along the lines of Ranger.'

She grinned right back at him, the two of them caught up in a moment too special to explain, too fragile to last as she wondered if it was too late to bolt into the forest and not look back.

Reluctant to break the spell but needing to before she said or did something silly, she jerked a thumb at the canoe. 'We use these on the tours?'

'Yeah, these babies allow the tourists to get as close to the glacier as possible.' He held out a hand to her. 'Hop aboard.'

Grateful for the helping hand, she clambered over the side and adjusted to the gentle rocking, hoping she didn't end up face-planting in the water.

'Scoot over, I'll sit next to you.'

She glanced around in surprise; there were enough vacant seats in the boat for another six people.

'To maintain the balance.'

His lips quirked in a naughty smile, the devilish glint in his eyes the same spectacular ice-blue as the glacier in front of him, alerting her to the fact his reasons for sitting next to her were far from practical.

As he settled next to her on the thin wooden plank, she tried to ignore the rub of his hard thigh against her own. Slivers of desire pierced her veins, sharp, bordering on painful, rendering her powerless against this guy and how he made her feel.

She took a calming breath, only to be swamped by his tantalising outdoorsy aftershave again, the one that short-circuited every self-preservation mechanism.

'We'll use the motor engine. Unless you feel like rowing?'

She shook her head as he shrugged out of his parka and laid it on the seat behind him, the simple action pulling his jumper tight across his chest, emphasising its breadth, its width, tempting her to touch...

As the engine roared to life and the canoe shot across the lake her fingers dug into the wooden seat. Grateful to have something else to focus on other than the tsunami of desire threatening to swamp and overturn every good intention she'd ever had of keeping him at bay, she focused on the breathtaking scenery, savouring the bracing frigid air slapping her cheeks.

He cut the engine as they neared the glacier face and the canoe drifted, allowing her to absorb the significance of what she saw in silence, the occasional bump of an ice chunk against the hull the only sound to disrupt the quiet.

She marvelled at the intense indigo of the ice as it contrasted with the polished granite walls and could hardly believe the size of the awesome ice as it tumbled from its mountainous height to the lake below. A cold wind suddenly sprung up, settling over her like a damp cloak.

Rhys noticed her shiver, picked up his parka and draped it across her shoulders. 'Better?'

Rather than stopping, her shudders intensified, though not from the cold. Being snuggled into his warm parka, his seductive scent imbedded into it, she wanted to snuggle in and never come up for air.

Then she made the mistake of glancing up while he was adjusting the parka, reaching across the front of her to pull the collar tight and secure it, his warm breath fanning her cheek, his lips inches away.

Her eyelids slammed shut as she concentrated on cold things in an effort to counteract the heat generated by his nearness: *Think freezers, think Arctic winters, think snowstorms.*

It didn't help.

With a resigned sigh, she opened her eyes, looked into his and did a spontaneous, crazy thing she knew she'd live to regret.

She kissed him.

Took the decision out of his hands by locking her arms around his neck, tipping her chin up, brushing her lips across his in the hope she'd send any last fleeting resistance straight to the bottom of the lake.

A soft sigh fell from her lips, seemed to galvanise him into action. His mouth devoured her, demanding a submission she was more than willing to give. She parted her lips, allowing his tongue full access to her craving mouth. Their tongues met in a sinuous dance, winding around each other in an endless quest for pleasure.

'This isn't a good idea,' he muttered, easing back a fraction. 'Says who?'

She kissed him again, not giving him time to protest further. This was wrong, so wrong; then why did it feel like the best thing that had happened to her in a long time?

She'd yearned for his kiss since last night, yet the reality far surpassed expectation. He kissed how he looked; like a dream, and she never wanted to wake up.

She held his head, her fingers splayed through his hair, pulling him closer. The silky strands teased her fingertips and she wanted to feel the rest of him. Hell, she wanted to run her hands over every last inch of him and come back for more.

With a reluctant groan he slipped his arms around her, his touch heating her better than any fire could. She leaned into him, fused to his body as she melded against him. Her body burned, her passion igniting with the skilled touch of his lips, his hands. She was a bonfire just waiting to happen. Just her luck he'd lit the match.

She'd never found her breasts particularly erogenous, though they ached for his touch, her erect nipples rubbing against the lacy confines of her bra. As if reading her mind, he slipped a hand under her jumper.

'That's so good,' she whispered against the side of his mouth, the soft, breathy sound at one with the serenity surrounding them in a sensual cocoon.

He growled, a low, guttural sound that echoed in the silence as his lips blazed a trail of hot, moist kisses from her ear to the hollow of her throat, as his hand cupped her breast and started to massage. Her world almost exploded as his thumb brushed across a sensitised nipple, the nub aching for his touch. As she edged closer to him, her newly awakened breasts craving his mouth with every passing second, the canoe started to rock wildly.

He pulled away and stared at her, wide-eyed, stunned, his dazed expression reflecting hers.

'A cold shower mightn't be a bad idea right about now, but a dunk in this icy water's probably taking things too far?'

'Agreed.'

She had no idea how long they stared at each other, their ragged breathing the only sound before he turned away on the pretext of fiddling with the engine.

How did he do that—just turn off? She was still seeing stars.

She scuttled across the seat away from him, adjusting her jumper self-consciously and wishing she could think of something funny to say as he restarted the engine. An uncomfortable silence grew, punctuated by the spluttering engine.

'That was a first.'

Stupidly, she said the first thing that popped into her head and he looked at her as if she'd gone mad, not knowing if she referred to the canoe, the glacier or that scintillating kiss.

As she tried not to cringe only one thought echoed through her head.

It's going to be a long six months.

CHAPTER EIGHT

AFTER his monumental error in judgement on the canoe a few moments ago, Rhys needed to take his frustrations out on something. Right this very minute, he was looking at her.

'You said you wanted to be one of the boys, right?'

Jade's tongue flicked out to moisten her bottom lip, a kick in his libido following that stupid kiss. 'Right.'

'Then you need to bring all the life jackets from the top shed down here, make sure they're all shipshape and store them in the locker over there. Think you can do it?'

He saw the flicker of doubt in her eyes, hoped she'd renege, capitulate. Then he'd have a legit excuse to fire her cute ass.

But before he could add to the challenge, she squared her shoulders, nodded. 'Need anything else while I'm up there?'

'Nope, just make it quick. We've got loads more to do.'

She hovered, her indecisiveness a clear indication she wanted to rehash that kiss and…what? Make excuses? Apologise? Ease the tension like last night in Skagway?

He turned his back before she could say anything, relieved when he heard her boots crunching on the gravel leading back to the path.

Waiting until he couldn't hear her footsteps, he finally exhaled his pent-up frustration in a long, low curse. Jamming his hands into his parka pockets—the damn thing now smelt of her, thanks to his stupid chivalry—he started pacing the shore, kicking at stones, scuffing his boots.

He'd seriously screwed up out there.

She might have initiated that kiss, but he should've stopped it. He'd wanted to do the right thing, had almost pulled away, but something in her eyes had slammed into him where he least expected or wanted it. Deep down in a place he didn't acknowledge existed any more.

He understood. Some jerk had done a number on her, she was on the rebound, wanting to assert her femininity, make sure she was still attractive and he happened to be the handiest guy around.

What he didn't understand was his reaction.

Had he lost his mind? The last time he'd kissed a woman out here there had been disastrous consequences, the reason he hadn't been back.

So what the hell was he doing?

Aiming a vicious kick at a large rock, he almost welcomed the stab of pain as he stubbed his toe. Anything to detract from the other pain; the pain of remembrance and how his careless actions had led to the death of a woman he cared about.

'Here's the first lot.'

Stunned, he turned to find Jade staggering down the path laden with enough lifejackets to outfit two canoes. He would've laughed if he weren't so disgusted with himself.

He should help her, should get the boys to pitch in, but he wanted her to fail this test, wanted her to find it exhausting.

Hating himself more with every step away from her, he jerked a thumb towards the lockers. 'Store them in there for now, get the rest, then do the inspection.'

Her mutinous glare had him crossing his fingers within his parka pockets but rather than stomp or yell—or, better, quit—she sent him a mocking salute before trudging back up the path into the forest.

Calling himself every name under the sun, he started checking the canoes, something the boys would do later, but needing to keep busy in an effort not to help Jade when she reappeared.

Determined not to crack, he kept his head down each time he heard her, four trips in all, his hands aching from clenching in the effort not to assist.

When she squatted next to the locker and started inspecting the life jackets, he risked a glance and his heart twisted.

She was a mess, her face flushed an angry pink and covered in perspiration, her hair frizzy and bristling, her lips cracked from the cold.

As if sensing his guilt, she looked up, her gaze defiant, daring him to admit he'd been a bastard because of what had happened between them.

Instead, he stood, dusted off his hands and crossed to the locker, sat on a nearby log and pointed at the pile of jackets.

'Better keep going. We haven't got all day.'

She bit her lip, obviously swallowing a host of retorts, before clamping her mouth shut and refocusing.

That was when it hit him.

The pampered princess had guts. Grit and determination and the drive to really make a go of this.

He would've valued those traits in any other employee, had seen them in Claudia…but he didn't want to compare her to Claudia, knew any slight similarities would only serve to make him harder on her.

After the way she'd handled her first test, she didn't deserve that.

He had the problem, not her. It wasn't just the kiss that had him so rattled. Uh-uh, it had started around the time he saw the genuine appreciation for this place in her eyes, her awestruck expression that told him she got it, that there was no place on earth as special as this.

Maybe he'd misjudged her? Was there more to the Princess than met his appreciative eyes? Only one way to find out.

'What happened in Sydney?'

Jade stiffened, her fingers convulsing around the straps of the life jacket she was checking.

She'd rather discuss that cringe-worthy kiss where she'd more than embarrassed herself than rehash her past.

'Nothing as important as getting this job done.'

She continued running her fingers along the straps, almost jumping out of her skin when he laid a hand on hers.

'Leave them. I'll get the boys to finish up.'

Snatching her hand out from under his on the pretext of standing, she shoved off the locker and put some distance between them.

'What's this? I passed your test so now we move on to the next stage, interrogation?'

She expected him to bristle, to instantly retreat. Instead, his wry smile eased the tension lines around his mouth.

'Fair call.'

He pointed to the life jackets. 'You passed, by the way. Fastest time on record too.'

'I ran all the way.'

Her calf and thigh muscles twanged to underline the fact. Knowing her luck, she wouldn't be able to walk for days.

'That's nuts.'

'Only way to prove to you I'm not some weak female playing winter dress-ups in the wild.'

'I never thought that.'

She shook her head. 'Don't lie. You have this tense muscle thing in your neck going on when you do.'

To her amazement a faint blush stained his cheeks. 'If I know what's motivating you to be here, maybe I won't be so tough on you.'

'Don't do me any favours,' she muttered as a spasm shot up her back and she bit back a groan.

He wouldn't give up. She could see it in every stubborn line of his body. Fine. She'd give him the abbreviated version.

Easing onto a log and trying not to wince, she folded her arms on top of her knees and rested her chin on top.

'I had a glittering social life in Sydney. Rich family. Only kid. All the perks.'

Or so she'd thought, until she'd confronted those closest to her and the world as she knew it came crashing down around her diamond-studded ears.

'You didn't like it?'

Her forced chuckle sounded bitter. 'I liked it just fine. Lapped it up from a young age, enjoyed all the trimmings.'

'So what made you leave it all behind?'

'I told you, my fiancé cheated on me.'

'Your *fiancé*?'

She nodded, absent-mindedly rubbed the base of her left ring finger where Julian's three-carat rock had resided; until she'd flung it at him on her way out of the door of his multimillion-dollar Double Bay mansion.

'All seemed so natural. Exit finishing school, enter perfect guy hand-picked by Daddy.'

'You were coerced into an engagement?'

She shook her head, remembering the first time she'd met Julian. How she'd been blown away by his manners and chivalry and polished good looks; how he'd made her innocent heart pitter-patter with his practised kisses; how he'd made her feel as she'd felt her whole life: cherished.

What a crock.

'Nothing like that. My dad moves in posh circles, so did Julian. He introduced us, we hit it off.'

Hugging her knees tighter, she blinked back the sting of bitter tears. 'The usual boring story. Whirlwind courtship. Magical proposal. All very glamorous and exciting and...'

'And?'

'Fake, the lot of them—it,' she amended, but not before she'd seen his raised eyebrow.

'Them?'

She shook her head. Discussing Julian with Rhys was bad enough. Having to tell him the whole sordid story of how she discovered her fiancé was a rat? No way.

'My parents are into the whole appearances thing, too. I've had a gutful.'

'So this job is an escape route? A whim to temporarily take your mind off it?'

She frowned at his judgement. 'You think I'm running away. I prefer to call it getting a much-needed wake-up call. Time to follow my own dreams rather than living up to the expectations of other people's.'

His jaw clenched as he absent-mindedly rubbed it, piquing

her curiosity. By all accounts he was footloose and fancy-free. What would he know about living up to others' expectations?

'Once I gain my biology degree, sky's the limit. I want to travel the world, researching the ecology and physiology of plant and animal species. Ideally, I'd love to prepare environmental impact reports for industry and government. You know, make a real difference.'

The reluctant admiration in his gaze made her want to preen. 'Can't fault you there. One of the reasons I became a park naturalist was to make a difference. I used to survey various parks, determining forest conditions and the distribution of fauna and flora, conferring with local councils on preserving a park. I loved it.'

He glanced around, his eyes drawn to the glacier shimmering in the distance. 'That's why I started my own tour company, so I could share a small, unique part of this beauty with people who might appreciate it, even if they only saw one tenth of what I did.'

Jade stared, mesmerised by the animation in his face as he spoke about his work. She'd never seen this side of him and it surprised her.

'Which parks did you work at?'

'You name the park, I've probably worked there. Started at Acadia National Park in Maine, moved on to White Mountain National Forest in New Hampshire where I used to lead a four-mile hike up Champney Falls Trail to the summit of Mount Chocorua.'

He screwed up his eyes, dredging up memories she sat forward to hear. She'd never seem him like this: blue eyes glowing yet unfocused, lost in reminiscing, his mouth relaxed, his hands animated.

'Then there was Great Smoky Mountains National Park in North Carolina. From the summit of LeConte Mountain you could see the amazing fall colours of maples, beeches and oaks in the valley below. It was awesome.'

'The only hike I've ever done in the States was in Yosemite. About six miles up to Vernal-Nevada Falls and I still remember the beauty of the dogwoods and maples covering the valley floor.'

He must've heard the wistful yearning in her voice. 'Sure you want to hear me rave on?'

She nodded, wriggling her fingers in a give-me-more gesture.

'Okay, you asked for it.' He held up his fingers, ticked points off. 'Throw in Chippewa National Forest in Minnesota, Targhee National Forest in Idaho and my Alaskan adventures and there you have it, my complete park naturalist CV.'

'So why did you swap that for a desk, if you loved it that much?'

He avoided her eyes, staring out over the vista instead. 'You know why.'

'Work-place accidents happen all the time. That shouldn't stop you.'

Shadows shifted in all that deep blue.

'I needed a change.'

He swept his arm to encompass the stunning vista in front of them. 'This will always be here. I can come back any time I want.'

His defiant declaration challenged her to deny his claim. She didn't. There was more behind his reticence to return to the wilderness he loved and while she harboured her own secrets it'd be unfair to push him to reveal his.

'Speaking of heading back, I need a long, hot bath before my muscles seize.'

Seeing another side to him, hearing the passion for nature in his voice—a passion that matched her own—only served to draw her closer, something she couldn't afford after that kiss. A kiss they hadn't talked about and for now she'd like to keep it that way.

'You did good, by the way.'

His gruffness was underlined by admiration and she smiled.

'Thanks, Ranger. I'm made of sterner stuff than you think.'

Pity a cramp in her calf had her tumbling off the log as she tried to stand, making a mockery of her declaration. She bit her lip, unsure whether to laugh or cry.

'Easy does it.'

Her pride took a well-earned rest as he helped her up and with a muttered 'Thanks,' she headed for the path.

She should be mad at him for putting her through that stupid test, should be angry at his lack of faith in her abilities.

However, as she hit the path and her legs silently protested at the increasing incline, she knew the build-up of lactic acid in her screaming muscles wasn't half as dangerous as the build-up of a monster crush on her boss.

CHAPTER NINE

JADE winced as she tweezed the last splinter from her hands, flexing her fingers and wishing she hadn't when the latest blister popped.

With a self-pitying sigh, she rummaged in the first-aid kit, doused the blister in antiseptic before sticking a Band-Aid across it, another to add to her collection.

She managed a wry grin as she studied her hands at arm's length, hands once treated to a French manicure on a weekly basis and now resembling something from a horror film with her split and cracked nails, calloused palms and multi-plastered fingers.

Not that she minded. These hands were testament to days of hard work, where she'd groomed trails, cleared forest growth and chopped wood.

While she'd been walking like a saddle-sore cowboy for days, and her muscles continued to protest, the fact she'd tackled every task gave her a sense of satisfaction she'd never imagined.

It hadn't been easy, far from it. Working in the wilderness was nothing like the gentle hikes through the Blue Mountains that she'd loved, or exploring ice caves in the Alps.

She'd always adored the cold and, combined with her love of nature, Alaska was her dream destination. Mentally, she was on the page. Physically, her cosseted body had a lot of catching up, toughening up, to do.

Snapping the first-aid kit shut, she shoved it into her backpack, checked the next job on her list and frowned.

Time for some one-on-one time with the boss.

Her induction week had been manic, giving her little time to ponder the consequences of that mind-blowing kiss when she'd rocked the boat, literally. Thankfully, Cody and Jack had given her most of her training and she'd barely had time to assimilate one piece of information before being bombarded with another.

The guys were patient, Rhys less so. He had high standards, demanding nothing less than perfection. She could handle it. What she couldn't handle was his cool composure bordering on abruptness, as if that make-out session in the canoe never happened and he clearly blamed her for it.

When they'd talked about their mutual love of nature after the kiss, she'd harboured a hope they could forget it and move on. By his curt manner over the last week, he'd reverted to treating her as an employee, a recalcitrant one at that, rather than someone who understood what it meant for him to be back here.

Reaching the shed, she dropped her backpack, stretched out her kinked back muscles and donned her chipper professional mask, the one that had made her face ache with the effort over the last week since the 'kiss that shall not be discussed'.

He glanced her way with the briefest nod.

'Itinerary clear?'

His tone clipped, Rhys checked the wet-weather gear for the fifth time that morning.

Resisting the urge to roll her eyes, she nodded. 'That's only the hundredth time you've asked me.'

He lifted his head from the task at hand, his stare imperturbable. 'No harm in being prepared.'

'You can't always be prepared for every eventuality.'

'What would you know about it?'

Keeping her mouth shut would've been the smart thing to do, but she'd had a gutful of his unflappable attitude and his annoying ability to act as if nothing had ever happened between them.

'Plenty.'

She planted her hands firmly on her hips, staring him down, daring him to argue.

He straightened and she silently cursed for noticing how hot he looked: taupe trousers accentuated his long legs and a green polo shirt with the Wild Thing gold emblem, a bald eagle in flight over the left breast pocket, hugged his broad chest. The uniform did little to detract. If anything, the deep green highlighted his brooding dark looks to perfection.

'So, you think a week out here makes you an expert?' His eyes narrowed, a dangerous gleam in their indigo depths.

'No, though I think I've learned enough to be a competent performer.'

'This isn't a circus.'

'Hard to tell, what with you behaving like a clown.'

His mouth twitched before he frowned.

'Don't push me, Jade.'

His low voice rumbled like thunder on a stormy day and sounded just as threatening. She ignored the warning. She could handle whatever he dished up and more.

'Is that a threat?'

'No, it's a promise.'

He shrugged, turned away, as if their conversation was wasting his time.

'Then why are you acting as if nothing happened between us?'

He stiffened, her flyaway comment hitting him right between the shoulder blades if his rigid posture was anything to go by. Good. That meant she had his attention and maybe they could confront the proverbial giant bear lurking in the woods and move past this continual tension.

'I asked you a question.'

For a moment she thought he'd swivel back to face her when he shifted weight onto his other foot. Instead, he headed for a nearby shelter and started checking the endless rows of plastic overalls.

'We've got work to do.'

She should leave it alone, leave him alone. But she couldn't stand another day of his offhand treatment, let alone another week.

Following him into the shelter, she picked up a clipboard and pen, ticking off inventory. When the frigid silence grew, she couldn't stand it any longer.

'Or maybe you've forgotten about it? All in a day's work—'

'Forgotten? I'm going crazy wanting a repeat performance.'

His blunt declaration knocked the wind out of her as she scrambled for something to say, something other than, 'I want a repeat too.'

'Oh.'

He raked a hand through his hair while she dragged in a few breaths, her earlier sass depleted. This was where prodding a grizzly got her: sore and sorry from being bitten.

'Look, I'm not an idiot. There's a spark between us. I've just got enough happening without added complications.'

He couldn't meet her eyes, his pained expression making her want to reach out despite being labelled a 'complication'.

'Problems?'

'Apart from you?'

His wry grin didn't ease the caution in his eyes.

'Something with the upcoming tour? Anything I can do to help?'

He shook his head, his jaw clenched. 'I need to handle this myself.'

It hit her like ice calving off a glacier. What was really bugging him, and she could've slapped herself upside the head for not realising sooner.

'The first tour's coming up—must be hard on you after what happened on your last trip out here.'

An employee had died and she'd left it alone in the aftermath of their kiss and her rigorous training schedule.

It stood to reason he'd be nervous and if that was the reason he hadn't been back here since…heck, he was probably going through some major stuff.

He flipped through the plastic overalls as she stepped in front of him. 'Tell me.'

'In the past. Let's leave it there.'

'We could, but I reckon you're on some kind of guilt trip over that death. Might help to talk about it?'

'Don't you ever quit?'

She tilted her chin up, used the stare she'd given Julian when she'd told him what he could with his three-carat diamond engagement ring.

'Not in my vocab. So what happened?'

The respect in his eyes made her feel as if she'd just gained a promotion.

'You're not going to give up 'til I tell you?'

'Damn straight.'

'Fine.'

He jammed his hands into his pockets, jerked his head towards a nearby bench hewn from pine.

'Claudia had worked the tours for a year, thought she knew everything backwards. Other employees said she was a know-all, overconfident, but I let it slide because she was damn good at her job. I used to do regular tours in those days...'

He trailed off, pain pinching his mouth. She stayed silent, giving him time, trying to ignore the warning signs that his audible agony, his obvious devastation, were more than that for a lost employee.

'Certain glaciers are off-limits. Claudia knew the ones but ignored the rules, wanted to get some hot pics for an article she was writing for a travel mag.'

Running a hand across his jaw, he turned to face her, his bleak expression clutching her heart.

'She rowed out, climbed onto the glacier, got killed in an avalanche.'

'I'm sorry.'

She reached out, covered his hand with hers, half expecting him to jerk away, surprised when he turned his palm over and clasped hers like a lifebuoy.

'Coroner's investigation cleared the company of any liability, but it was my fault—'

'No!'

She squeezed his hand, so tight he had no option but to look at her.

'I should've reined her in. Read the Riot Act, done something.'

He shook his head, guilt narrowing his eyes. 'Want to know why I didn't?'

She knew it was a rhetorical question, waited for his answer.

'Because she was a crazy rebel who reminded me of me. I was that daredevil who pushed boundaries, who climbed higher or skied steeper or swam out farther than anyone else. I admired her. Hell, I wanted to race her there and back.'

His voice shook with emotion and in that instant she had her suspicions confirmed. Claudia had been more than an employee and while a small, irrational part of her refused to be jealous of a dead woman, the rest of her couldn't help but resent how darn wonderful the adventurous woman must've been for him to still mourn her.

Running a hand over his face didn't erase his bleak expression. 'She knew I admired her recklessness, seemed to grow wilder as…time passed. She was up for anything.'

She didn't want to know what that pause meant, her curious mind already filling in the blanks: *as they'd grown closer, as they'd started a relationship, as they'd planned for a future.*

As for Claudia being 'up for anything'…yep, she needed a topic change fast before she turned any greener.

Releasing his hand, she patted it, hoping to convey her understanding, her sympathy.

'But you were smarter than that. She made her choice and, unfortunately, not the best one. That can never be your fault.'

He stared into her eyes for a priceless moment before he straightened, his lips compressed, his expression resolute.

'This stays strictly between us.'

'Of course.'

Predictably, he stood and grabbed his clipboard. He'd opened up to her, more than she could've hoped for, and that meant he'd now retreat. It was what he'd done from the first moment they'd sparked.

'Let's get back to work.'

With a resigned sigh she stood, laid a hand on his arm, felt him stiffen beneath it.

'Thanks for trusting me enough to tell me the truth.'

She wasn't surprised when he stalked away.

Jade's first tour went off without a hitch. The tourists were eager to learn about the Alaskan wilderness and viewed her as an expert. Who was she to disillusion them? She expounded information on the local flora and fauna like a native Alaskan, relaying information she'd absorbed like a sponge earlier that week. Predictably, the tourists were just as gobsmacked at their first glimpse of Davidson Glacier as she'd been.

Once the last tourist boarded the JetCat for the return journey to Skagway she finally relaxed, sank to her haunches and exhaled, watching the catamaran sail into the distance.

Cody slapped her on the back and she almost overbalanced. 'Nice going. Jack and I better lift our act otherwise you'll be doing us out of a job.'

'Doubt that.' She took hold of his outstretched hand as he pulled her to her feet. 'I'm exhausted.'

'It gets easier.' He smiled, jerked his head behind her. 'Besides, I doubt you're the only one feeling the pinch. The boss looks beat. He's out of practice.'

As Cody released her hand, she turned and saw Rhys striding towards them, his expression grim.

'Don't worry about old grizzly. His bark is far worse than his bite. I'm outta here. Better give Jack a hand doing the final check on the canoes for tomorrow.'

Her concern for how Rhys had coped on his first tour after Claudia's death was overshadowed by Cody's words conjuring up a vision of Rhys nibbling at her neck, just as he'd done on the canoe, and she blushed.

'Cody's lines working like a charm?'

Rhys's posture screamed tension, from the stiffness of his shoulders to the rigid neck muscles. Guess that answered the question of how he'd coped today.

'He was just saying what a good job I did today.'

He nodded. 'He's right. You were good, better than I expected.'

'Thanks, I think.'

'You look tired. How do you feel?'

'A bit sore, actually. I'm not used to hiking up and down slippery forest trails with two-hundred-pound women holding on to my coat-tails for support.'

She held her breath as he smiled, the first time she'd seen his lips curve upwards since that revealing chat when he'd shared more than she'd expected.

'Forgot to warn you about that.'

She shrugged, wincing as she did so. 'Guess you can't be prepared for everything out here, especially the *frailties* of women who have been feasting on lavish four-course dinners on cruise ships for the last week and then deciding they need a helping hand when the going gets tough.'

He laughed as she rolled her shoulders gingerly, surprised at how quickly the muscles had stiffened. After the harrowing physicality of the last week, she'd expected to be fitter. Too bad her muscles weren't as developed as her overactive imagination as she constantly spun scenarios of how involved Rhys and Claudia had been.

'Should I help the guys with the canoes or do you want me to clean up the lunch hut?'

Surprise skated across his eyes before he blinked, shook his head. 'You've done enough today. Head back, take a long soak, okay?'

She nodded, biting back a whimper of pain too late as concern compressed his lips.

'Here, let me help.'

He spun her around, started kneading the knotted muscles, slowly, rhythmically. She bit back a groan, let her head flop forward, providing him with better access to her aching muscles while valiantly trying to ignore how incredibly seductive his hands would feel all over.

'That feels *so* good.'

She'd forgive him his bizarre interview technique, his aborted kiss in Skagway and his walking away from her when they'd started to bond this morning, as long as his hands continued to work their magic.

She'd had therapeutic massages at Sydney's top day spa, a Javanese Lulur at a five-star Balinese resort and a combination Swedish massage at London's finest hotel, yet none had felt as good as this.

With his hands this masterful, she had a whole range of places aching for his soothing touch.…

Rhys bit his lip in frustration, the feel of Jade's firm sinews beneath his hands combined with her soft moans driving him crazy. As if he hadn't spent the last week taking cold showers in an attempt to cool his passion.

He knew why he'd started this: guilt. She'd been an absolute trouper over the last week, following orders, giving her all, and even when she must have ached all over her hot little body she'd asked if he had any more jobs for her to do.

That took guts, determination, qualities he admired, qualities he identified with. That alone should send him running, and along with the fact she now knew more about him than anyone— courtesy of their little revealing tête-à-tête this morning—should have him avoiding her at all costs.

Yet here he was, his hands platonically soothing when they'd like to be something else entirely. Doing this out of chivalry and guilt were one thing, putting himself through this torture another.

For no matter his therapeutic intentions, to ease some of her soreness for being such a team player, the instant he'd touched her, his libido had roared.

Ignoring something didn't make it go away—he should know that better than anyone—and their first kiss had merely served to stoke the fire. Her silky mouth, warm and welcoming, and the feel of her luscious breasts had haunted him every day and night since. He'd stayed away from her deliberately, allowing Jack and Cody to instruct her on the finer points of leading the tours, but it hadn't eased his libido.

Then he'd had to go and dump all that heavy stuff about Claudia on her this morning, divulging way more than intended. That should've been a libido killer but offloading some of the guilt he'd been feeling, verbalising it, had only served to increase his need for her.

She'd been right; he'd been nervous as hell. Not just by the thought of returning to the scene of Claudia's death, but being confronted by a sexy woman wearing his company's emblem over her left breast and battling the constant urge to sweep her into his arms, stride into the house and hole up with her in there for the next week.

Massaging her had been pure reflex reaction; seeing her in obvious pain had brought out his dormant chivalrous side.

Yeah, right. Real chivalrous when all he could think about was continuing the massage all over her sexy body, stroking her until she cried his name.

'That feels *so-o-o* good, Rhys,' she murmured, his name on her lips inciting all sorts of vivid visions of her screaming his name during sex.

Increasingly uncomfortable with his thoughts heading down a one-way track to erotica, he shuffled, causing her to lose her footing slightly and slide back, smack bang against his hard-on.

He silently cursed yet didn't move, curious to see what her reaction would be. His hands didn't stop, alternately stroking and kneading as he wondered if she'd run screaming into the woods or turn around and make his day.

'Mmm…better,' she murmured, a hint of smug amusement in her voice as she wriggled her butt against his erection, driving him crazy.

The little minx! He was on the verge of losing control and she was actually enjoying it.

'Feeling tense, Ranger? Would you like me to return the favour?'

She turned slowly as he clamped down on the urge to shove her up against the nearest tree and bury himself in her heat.

'What did you have in mind?'

'Whatever you want.'

The overwhelming need to possess her rumbled deep within as she stared at him with those half fearful, half expectant brown eyes, a seductive contrast of innocence and vixen.

Her words might be wanton, but her body didn't lie. He'd had women come on to him and that was exactly what they did: drape themselves over him, press their breasts against him, use their hands to titillate.

Jade did none of those things. She just stood there, lips parted, cheeks flushed, dark eyes darting yet unable to hide the glitter of desire.

He should do the noble thing, put this down to her excessive tiredness. But where was the fun in that?

He deliberately stared at her lips until she flicked her tongue out to moisten them, that one little dart hitting him straight in the groin.

'Some areas of my body are tenser than others.'

He heard her sharp intake of breath, watched her pupils dilate, expecting her to run.

When she tilted her chin up, eyeballed him and said, 'Let me touch you,' his libido rocketed to the top of the glacier without a hope of coming down any time soon.

'Hey, you two ready for dinner?'

The sexual haze embracing them shattered in an instant, Jack's booming voice dousing them like a bucket of icy water, and they leaped apart.

'Stand in front of me.'

With a quick glance at the bulge in his trousers, her blush deepened as she shifted position to cover his front.

'Be right there, just debriefing after my hectic first day.'

'Stop gasbagging and hurry up. Dinner's served and I'm starving.'

Rhys muttered, 'He's not the only one.'

She laughed and turned to face him. 'He's talking about food. How long since you've had a date anyway?'

'Too long if my reaction to you is any indication.' He thrust his hands into his pockets, which only drew her attention back to his groin, her curious gaze not helping the situation. At this rate he wouldn't be able to walk.

'Yeah, I can see that.'

She dragged her gaze away from his groin, travelled upwards at a leisurely pace, her slow perusal making him want to puff out his chest in pride. 'Care to tell me what's going on?'

'Well, it's fairly simple really. When a man finds a woman attractive, some of his extremities take on a life of their own. I think they call it an erec—'

'Thanks for the biology lesson, but with my interest in the subject I'm well aware how mammals function.'

He enjoyed sparring with her, had liked how she'd been up for the challenge during her interview and, now, admired how she didn't back down from his teasing.

'Maybe you should concentrate on plant life? Much less complicated.'

'Is that what this is to you? A complication?'

Her lips curved in a smile but he saw the quirk of uncertainty in her raised brow.

'Isn't it for you?'

She gnawed on her bottom lip as he battled the driving urge to do the same. 'I came here to work and learn as much as I can. I sure didn't count on…*this*.'

Her hand wavered between them and she didn't need to elaborate. He knew exactly what *this* was. *This* still had him so hard he could barely stand.

'Just so you know, whatever happens, it can't move past this. I'm not a stayer, never have been. There's no room in my life for a relationship.'

There, he'd laid it out for her, told her the cold, hard truth, given her a chance to run before *this* got even more complicated.

It was the only way, the fair way, for he'd be damned if he left here riddled with guilt a second time.

The gnawing stopped, only for her fingers to start twirling a strand of hair over and over.

'I'm not interested in a relationship either.' He only just caught her muttered, 'Not again in this lifetime.'

'Just so we're clear, no relationships, but what about—?'

'Come on, you two, grub's up!'

This time, he cursed Jack's interruption loudly and vociferously.

She smiled, glanced over his shoulder and held up a finger at Jack for a minute. 'Guess we better eat?'

He nodded, brushed a stray strand of hair out of her eyes. 'We'll finish this conversation when we're alone after the boys go into town next weekend.'

'Huh?'

'The supply trip. Didn't the boys mention it?'

He'd been thinking of nothing else, wondering how he'd keep his hands off her when they'd completed all their jobs and were left to socialise, the only two people out here.

Socialising could mean watching DVDs, sharing a meal, making small talk. But they'd moved way past all that with that kiss and the shared confidences, and it was that developing closeness that scared him more than anything.

Her forehead wrinkled adorably in concentration before she nodded. 'Yeah, they did say something. I forgot.'

'Perhaps a case of selective memory? Maybe you didn't like the thought of being alone with me so you blocked it out?'

She shook her head, strands of her loose ponytail whipping between them. 'Maybe I was looking forward to it so much I didn't want it to distract from my work?'

He laughed, finding her familiar pluck as stimulating as the rest of her, placed a hand in the small of her back as they headed up the hill. 'Good call.'

'Can I make another?'

'Sure?'

Glancing at him from beneath lowered lashes, a sexy smile curving her kissable lips, she said, 'Rest up for the remainder of the week, conserve energy. Come the weekend, Ranger, you're going to need it.'

CHAPTER TEN

'HURRY up, you big oaf. We're going to miss the boat.' Cody nudged Jack with his elbow; he seemed hell-bent on moving at tortoise speed.

'Sounds like the story of my life,' Jade mumbled as she helped tidy up the breakfast dishes.

'Pardon, mate?' Cody winked.

'Lose the Ockerisms. I'm in the States now so enough of your Crocodile Dundee jokes, your "throw another shrimp on the barbie, mate" and the "thunder from Down Under" comments.'

Cody laughed. 'Someone's a bit testy this morning. Perhaps the thought of spending quality time alone with the boss has you all riled up?'

She concentrated on rubbing a non-existent spot off a plate, hoping she wasn't that transparent. 'Why would you say that?'

'I see the way you two look at each other. If there were any more sparks this forest would be in danger of going up in smoke.'

An embarrassing blush crept into her cheeks and she ducked her head, ditching the plate to scour a frying pan instead.

'Don't know what you're talking about.'

Jack joined in Cody's guffaws. 'We think it's kinda neat, the two of you mooning around.'

She scrubbed harder.

'And it's not like the boss-man has done this before. Well, at least not since…'

Cody sent Jack a death glare as he jumped in with, 'Just so you know, he doesn't have a girl in every igloo.'

Jack rushed on. 'But you know he's a confirmed bachelor, right?'

'Yeah,' Cody piped up. 'We wouldn't want you getting your hopes up or anything.'

Enough. The pan clattered from her hands, making an almighty racket in the sink as she turned to face the guys, sudsy hands on hips.

'Isn't it time you left?'

Their teasing grins slipped. 'Hey, we're just kidding around. You're okay, right?'

She nodded, poked her tongue at them. 'Guess I'm lucky, having you two bozos looking out for me.'

Cody and Jack high-fived. 'Damn straight.'

Footfalls outside the kitchen had the guys shrugging into their backpacks double time.

With an exaggerated wink, Cody saluted her. 'Now remember, don't do anything I wouldn't do.'

As Rhys entered the kitchen they waved and beat a hasty retreat.

'What was that about?'

Rhys jerked his head towards the departing guides, a bemused expression on his face.

'Boys being boys.'

He reached for a tea towel, started drying the plates, the sight of him engaged in a domestic chore bringing an unexpected lump to her throat. Or did that have more to do with the fact he'd probably done this before, with Claudia?

Hearing the boys articulate what she'd already gleaned from the little info he'd shared with her made her incredibly sad. Female employees out here weren't common, she knew that, so did that make her a convenience? An inevitable attraction?

And hearing the fact the boys knew of his involvement with Claudia added a whole new dimension to his guilt. If they were seriously involved, did that mean losing her had closed him off emotionally?

'I think our young tour guides have a crush on you.'

Plonking a frying pan in the sink with enough vigour to raise his eyebrow, she muttered, 'Not likely.'

The way she reacted whenever Rhys was near, it was more likely she was the one with a stupid crush.

'As long as the feeling's not mutual?'

She smirked at his question, a small part of her wishing he'd asked out of jealousy before remembering his anti-fraternising-employees policy—which obviously didn't include them!

'What do *you* think?'

'I think you know exactly how you affect the male species.'

She loved the timbre of his voice: rich, deep, sensual. It reminded her of her favourite caramel chocolate, all smoothness and honey. And probably just as dangerous to her well-being as the chocolate was to her hips.

Flicking soap suds his way to distract from a growing blush, she rinsed her hands and dried them. 'Yep, that's me, a regular femme fatale.'

Glancing down at her moss-green jumper, black jeans and hiking boots, she nodded. 'Just give me a minute to slip into my diamonds and satin.'

He laughed. 'Any plans for today?'

'Not really. Thought I'd scout around the local area, check out the wildflowers.'

It would be her first chance to explore freely and she'd been looking forward to it all week. With the added bonus of keeping out of his way and away from the temptation of dragging him back to that canoe.

For all her earlier sassy bravado after his impromptu massage, she now had a serious case of nerves. Casually flirting to cover up her blossoming crush was one thing; now she had him alone a tiny part of her was scared. Scared she was in over her head, scared she might botch this and ruin her limited professional credibility in the process, scared she already liked him too much and was in danger of getting hurt.

'How about I show you some of the best spots?'

So much for avoiding temptation. Why didn't he just offer her the apple in paradise and be done with it?

He turned away and draped the tea towel over the oven handle, effectively preventing her from reading the expression on his face. Where had the invitation come from? Did he want to get her alone in the wilderness and go for a repeat performance on the lake or was he establishing distance by donning his professional park naturalist hat and giving her a tour?

Whatever his motivation, her heart raced at the thought of spending time alone with him.

'Sure, sounds good. Thanks for the offer.'

'You're welcome.'

His slow-burning smile sent a quiver of anticipation through her, the stacked plates in her hands making a giveaway rattle.

'Do I need to bring anything?'

If his sexy smile did wicked things to her insides, it had nothing on the briefest touch of his knuckles running gently down her cheek.

'Just yourself.'

The plates barely made it into the cupboard in one piece.

Jade sketched, desperate to capture the intense colours of the flowers. Her fingers flew over the paper, reproducing the exact shape and colour of the Arctic forget-me-not, the Tundra rose and the bell-heather flower, oblivious to Rhys's presence until he tapped her on the shoulder.

'Hey, remember me?'

She looked up from her sketchpad, startled at his close proximity. 'Sorry, I've been so caught up I forgot you were here.'

He clutched his heart. 'Ouch! My ego's wounded.'

She laughed at his antics. 'Your ego's big enough. I'm sure a dent here or there wouldn't affect it that much.'

Grimacing, he rubbed the chest area over his heart. 'Nope, still smarting. What did I do to deserve this?'

She swatted him on the arm. 'I don't know, but *you* hired *me*, remember?'

'How could I forget?'

His voice deepened and her pulse took off at the predictable rate whenever he so much as glanced her way.

She shivered at the recollection of her interview. It had only been a few weeks yet her first impression of her sexy boss hadn't dulled. If anything, her feelings had intensified. Frighteningly so.

Ignoring her thudding heart, she quickly changed the subject. 'What do you think of these?'

He studied her sketches. 'You're good. If the biology doesn't work out, you can always become an artist.'

'No way. I'm not creative enough for that.'

He stared directly into her eyes. 'I think you are.'

She looked away, wishing her heart would stop pounding like a teenager's every time he flirted with her.

'Here, I made you this.'

Rhys held out his hand. He had wound together a colourful chain of mountain flowers. She picked it up and inhaled, savouring the combination of sweet floral scents.

'Thanks, it's beautiful,' she murmured, wondering if she could press them.

She'd always been prone to sentimentality and had held on to keepsakes from past crushes. Pathetic. Thankfully, she'd kicked the habit with Julian and had thrown out every last card, letter and flower he had ever sent her.

Rhys plucked it out of her hand and placed the floral wreath on her head.

'Now it is.'

Their gazes locked, the silence crackling with a tangible heat.

'Not bad for a *cheechako*,' he said, his eyes burning with an emotion she couldn't begin to fathom.

She wrinkled her nose. 'I have the distinct impression you just called me a nasty name.'

'Would I do that?' His face was the picture of innocence. If she could call the devil innocent.

She merely raised an eyebrow.

'*Cheechako* is native Alaskan, means a tenderfoot trying

to survive their first year in Alaska. You're doing a good job. It can be tough with limited entertainment and only guys for company.'

She blushed, thinking the guy sitting before her had provided her with more entertainment than she could've wished for. And, yeah, it had been tough, looking at all that eye candy whenever he'd pulled off his shirt or squatted down when working. Real tough.

'Thanks. I love it out here. It's everything I could've hoped for.'

Looking around, she took in the sweeping mountain views, the endless azure sky, the lush, verdant landscape.

'Besides, entertainment is overrated.'

She didn't see his hand coming until it snaked across her sketchbook, captured hers.

'Is that why you love this place so much? It's the antithesis of your life in Sydney?'

Her startled gaze flew to his. 'How do you do that?'

'What?'

'Hone in on what I'm thinking.'

He shrugged, his smile bashful. 'I'm a man of many talents.'

Wasn't that the truth, his mind-reading being the least of them.

She stared at his hand over hers, so strong, the pads of his fingers calloused, making her skin tingle with the slightest abrasive scrape.

'You didn't answer my question.'

As she lifted her gaze from their joined hands and took in the spectacular view, drew a deep breath that filled her lungs with pure floral ambrosia, snuggled deeper into her anorak, she knew there was no place she'd rather be than here.

But it was more than Alaska and having his hand squeeze her gently in encouragement only served to increase the scary feeling expanding in her chest.

Rhys didn't want a relationship; he'd spelled it out. For all she knew he was still hung up on his dead girlfriend. Yet here, now, in the perfect stillness of a perfect moment, she wanted to share a small part of her nobody else saw.

'I love this place because it's simple. Sure, it's freezing, occasionally brutal on a newbie like me, but it's essentially honest.'

Turning her hand over, she slid her fingers between his. 'And yeah, you're right, that's the opposite of my life in Sydney.'

He searched her face for answers she had a feeling were clearly displayed. 'You're not just talking about your rat bastard fiancé, are you?'

Smiling at his apt description of Julian, she nodded. 'Don't get me wrong, I loved my life there, but when everything went pear-shaped, it's like I had the metaphorical blinkers ripped from my eyes. Everything seemed so clear...'

And that was what scared her the most: that she'd seriously loved Julian, had idolised her parents, had coasted through her cushy life, content to only see what she wanted to see.

She'd been so hung up on appearances, just like them, she'd lost sight of the stuff that really mattered, and lost a piece of herself in the process.

Her faith in her own judgement had taken a serious whack, making her doubt herself in so many ways. A doubt that crept over her now as Rhys squeezed her hand, released it, making her wonder if she'd said too much, had got too deep too quickly and scared him.

'Don't beat yourself up. At times we see what we want to see.'

He didn't look at her, his gaze fixed on a distant mountain, his jaw rigid.

'We're not just talking about me any more.'

Dejection tightened his features, his eyes despairing before he blinked, erasing a depth of feeling that staggered her.

'I just meant sometimes it's easier to drift along, seeing the good stuff, pretending the rest doesn't exist until it's too late—'

He stopped abruptly, as if he'd said too much, and leapt to his feet.

'I'm going fishing.'

Considering his lack of gear, fishing was a euphemism for escaping their discussion. Looked as if Ranger could add 'master of the quick bolt' alongside his impressive park naturalist qualifications.

'Hope they're biting.'

With a brisk nod, he stomped off into the forest while she gathered up her gear, managing a weary smile.

She'd been nervous about being alone with him out here for fear of a continuation of their hot make-out session.

Instead, she now had something even greater to fear: gaining more insight into a guy who now tugged on her emotions as well as her hormones.

Rhys trudged through the forest, mentally kicking himself.

What on earth possessed him to blab whenever he was alone with Jade?

Must be his libido messing with his head. The more he tried to ignore the spark between them, the more he veered towards a touchy-feely side he never knew existed.

Kicking at a tree root, he enjoyed the stab of momentary pain, distracting from a deeper, harsher pain he kept buried. The pain of loss, the pain of guilt, the pain of helplessness.

Losing Archie had introduced him to all those incredibly soul-destroying pains. Losing Claudia reinforced it.

She'd never been the love of his life—he'd need to have a heart to have one of those—far from it. The fiery redhead had been a daredevil, a kindred spirit, wild and carefree and totally living in the moment.

He'd identified with her, had lived vicariously through her when he'd had to play the responsible boss and she'd been free to indulge her wild streak.

They'd connected on so many levels. Until things got complicated. And he never did complicated.

Withdrawing had only served to push her towards that final day, the day he could barely think about for the weight of guilt crushing him.

Now there was Jade, all bright-eyed and enthusiastic and ready to tackle whatever Alaska threw her way.

While she wasn't as crazy or fearless as Claudia, the similarities were there: the willingness to prove herself, the eagerness to learn, the unbreakable spirit.

But there was far more depth to Jade. Her sensitivity, her caring, her ability to gently delve into areas he'd deliberately closed off from everyone, particularly himself.

He didn't want to open up to her.

He didn't want to like her.

What if it was too late?

Letting fly a curse, he broke into a small clearing near the river's edge, dragged in a breath and squeezed his eyes shut.

When he reopened them, took in the gurgling water tumbling over rocks, saw the flash of pink salmon darting low and the scattering of pale sunshine on the river's surface, he immediately calmed.

If Davidson Glacier was his favourite place on earth, this place was a close second.

Heading to his makeshift shed, he gathered his rod, bait and folding stool, plonking the lot next to the river.

He'd never had the patience for fishing, had hated anything sedentary when he'd rather be caving or abseiling or parachuting.

But those days were behind him and there was something infinitely calming about sitting next to flowing water with a rod in his hand, with nothing better to do than wait for a bite, alone with his thoughts.

As he settled on the stool, baited his hook and cast out, letting the welcome silence wash over him, he wondered at the wisdom of being here.

He could usually control his thoughts, keeping them away from random forays into the part of him locked away.

However, after another conversation with Jade fresh in his mind he couldn't do anything but think; about her.

His plan to keep busy, keep her working hard and ignore the attraction between them was failing miserably. If anything, the harder he pushed her, and seeing her struggle valiantly to keep up, only served to ratchet up his admiration.

As for their shared confidences, those little snippets of personal stuff they kept dragging out of each other…he'd never felt so close to anyone.

So what the hell was he going to do?

His first plan of keeping his distance wasn't working. Maybe he should go the other way? Get this *thing* for her out of his system. Lose the mystique, the fascination she held. What did he have to lose?

He'd already lost a piece of himself to her, opening up about Claudia, revealing more than he wanted anyone to know.

Perhaps focusing on the physical would obliterate his crazy need to confide in her the closer they grew?

But he'd persistently pushed her away; she'd think he was nuts if he did the opposite. Unless he showed her…

As his line grew taut and he concentrated on reeling in their dinner a glimmer of an idea worked its way into his muddled head.

Dinner…

Showing her…

Yeah, he was sick of all this talking they seemed to be doing.

Time for a little action.

CHAPTER ELEVEN

SEVERAL hours later Jade woke to the tantalising aroma of grilled salmon.

Her nose twitched as she sat up, rubbed her eyes and glanced at the time. Looked like her nana nap had turned into an exhausted two-hour siesta. Considering her lack of sleep lately, she must've needed it. No prizes for guessing the cause of her insomnia.

As if on cue, Rhys knocked on the door before opening it and sticking his head in. 'Dinner time, Sleeping Beauty.'

'Be there in a sec.'

Better make that an hour, she thought as she washed her face and ran a comb through her messy hair. After dumping Julian she'd had her thick hair layered, opting for a less extreme change than getting the lot hacked off. Considering it was now totally unruly, refusing to behave to any ministering whatsoever, maybe she should've gone with the GI Jane look.

With a slash of pale pink lip gloss, she was ready. Poking her tongue out at her reflection, she marvelled at the changes in herself. A few months ago she wouldn't set foot outside her palatial bedroom without a full face of make-up. Appearance had been everything. Unfortunately, she'd learned that the hard way.

Slamming the door on her memories, she headed for the main house, following the sounds of soft R & B from the living room.

Rhys had a thing for rhythm and blues. He also had a thing

for soaring ceilings, bleached pine boards and views for miles around if this room was any indication.

The first time he'd given her the grand tour and she'd stepped into here, her mouth had dropped. She'd visited ostentatious palaces and showy mansions in her time, but this place demonstrated money could be used for subtle class.

Modular ebony leather sofas and reclining chairs, thick rugs, and a modern steel-enclosed open fire added to the ambiance created by the ivory walls, high exposed beams and those floor-to-ceiling windows showing nature at its best.

It should've clashed amid the rugged wilderness outside but, somehow, this house and everything in it blended into the landscape, as if a giant hand had scooped out a chunk of mountain and nestled the house inside the hole, cradling it, nurturing it, approving.

'Hope you're hungry.'

He stepped into the room, silhouetted against a window, rivalling the view for breathtaking beauty.

'Starving.'

Helpless to stop her hammering heart, she sauntered towards the fire, where he'd laid out their dinner on a picnic rug.

She'd never had an indoor picnic, never done anything so wildly romantic, and it confused the heck out of her. When he'd stomped off on his *fishing* expedition earlier, she'd thought he'd retreat tonight. It wouldn't have surprised her in the least if he'd feigned a headache and eaten in his room.

Yet here he was, playing the charming host, laying out a romantic setting complete with music. What was he up to? As if he didn't bamboozle her enough without the trimmings.

'This looks delicious.'

'Thanks. Thought we'd dine informal tonight. Hope you don't mind?'

'Not at all.'

'Good.'

Her mouth watered as he handed her a plate filled with grilled herb-encrusted salmon steak, corn on the cob and a baked potato slathered in butter and chives, though she didn't know what made her salivate more. His impressive culinary skills or his impressive chest, every muscular ridge and bump highlighted in an azure shirt the same stunning colour of his eyes.

Heat surged to her cheeks—thankfully, she could blame it on proximity to the open fire—as she focused on her plate and not on the expanse of skin visible where his collar opened in a tantalising V.

'The fishing jaunt was a success, I see?'

'Never any doubt.'

Wisely, she kept her doubts that he'd even gone fishing to herself.

Biting into a succulent piece of salmon, she sighed. 'Aren't these rivers brimming with salmon? Bet this poor sucker practically leapt onto your hook.'

'Eat!' He growled, his eyes glinting with amusement.

They ate in relaxed silence and she savoured every mouthful, enjoying the luxury of having a man cook for her. Julian's idea of cooking had been ordering the caterers to stock the freezer with pre-cooked meals.

After she'd cleaned her plate, she sat back and patted her stomach.

'That was some dinner.'

He smiled, his teeth glowing in the reflected firelight.

'Wait 'til you see dessert.'

Jade gulped, unable to move as he reached over and took her plate, his hand brushing hers, sending sparks shooting from her fingertips to her toes. Their eyes locked and she could've sworn electricity sizzled in the air.

'Don't move. I'll be right back.'

Watching him stroll out of the room, faded denim clinging to his sensational butt, she wavered.

If she didn't move, she was in serious danger of falling flat on her back and yelling, 'Take me now!' when he came back.

If she moved, she'd miss out on all the fabulous stuff that would happen if she did fall flat on her back and yell, 'Take me now!'

Dilemmas, dilemmas…

He took the decision out of her hands, returning quickly with a platter of strawberries and melted chocolate.

'Oh, boy, you sure know the way to a girl's stomach,' she said, snaffling a strawberry and popping it in her mouth before he could set them down on the rug.

He paused, sent her a sizzling look. 'Maybe it's not the girl's stomach I'm after.'

The stomach in question belly-flopped at the intent in his eyes, her heart joining her tummy in an impressive somersault routine.

Thankfully, he turned away to tend to the fire and she leaned back, propped on outstretched arms, content to watch, loving the way the muted firelight played across the sharp angles of his face, how it shimmered orange against his Western shirt. Definite possibilities with that shirt, considering the pop buttons all the way down the front...

'That should keep us warm for a while.'

He sat next to her, his thigh barely inches from her own, a slow-building heat radiating between them. Or was it just the heat from the fire, with her imagination working overtime?

'Dessert?'

His low, husky voice rippled over her and before she could launch herself at him with a resounding yes, he offered her the platter of strawberries.

'Thanks, my favourite.'

Before she could pick one he chose the plumpest, juiciest strawberry, whisked it through the chocolate and offered it to her, hovering a hair's-breadth in front of her lips.

Guess this answered her earlier question of what was he doing. Every slow-motioned action, every glimmer in those too-blue eyes, every tilt of those sexy lips, screamed seduction.

After spending so many tense moments retreating from her, he'd finally decided to stop running. She should ponder why; why the sudden turnaround, why now, after he'd made it clear this wasn't a good idea.

But as he brushed the strawberry over her bottom lip in a slow, sensual sweep she wanted to lose herself in the moment and to hell with any questions.

Her eyes didn't leave his as she slowly opened her lips, moved a fraction and enclosed her mouth over the deliciously smooth chocolate tip.

She moaned, her eyelids drifting shut as she bit into the strawberry, savouring the explosion of sweet tanginess mingling with the luscious chocolate, her senses on overload as she took the whole fruit in her mouth, her tongue flicking out, only to encounter a fingertip.

She could've sworn Rhys's moan echoed hers, but as her eyes flew open he'd sat back, placing the tray within reaching distance if she wanted more. She'd never considered fruit erotic, but she sure as heck would view strawberries a whole lot different after tonight.

As she plucked another strawberry off the plate, popped it in her mouth, she sighed in contentment. He couldn't have planned a more lovely evening. So where did they go from here? Damned if she was going to fling herself at him again, which meant Ranger would have to make the first move.

The fire crackled and hissed and spluttered, punctuating the silence, as she shoved a few more strawberries into her mouth so she wouldn't have to speak.

'Want to hear a story?'

'Sure.'

Anything to distract from the temptation of sitting this close to a guy who had the potential to fulfil every one of her wildest fantasies.

'The Alaskan people believe strongly in their traditions. Each tradition has a purpose and this is one of my favourites. The Alaskan women always had long, beautiful hair. A woman in mourning would cut her hair short and wear tattered clothes. She would keep this up 'til her husband's *potlatch*, or burial ceremony, was over. Only then did she fix herself up again and think of marriage.'

She had the distinct impression there was a hidden meaning behind his story.

'Are you trying to tell me you can't move on from something in the past 'til you've buried it?'

He continued to stare into the fire. 'I just like the story. I can't imagine being that in love with anyone, let alone wanting to move on so soon after their death. Good luck to the people who find that kind of love.'

Silence descended, punctuated by the crackling of wood as the flames consumed it.

'Are you over Julian?'

His question came out of left field.

She turned to stare at the enigmatic man by her side.

'Where did that come from?'

He shrugged, still avoiding her gaze. 'Just wondered.'

'I'm well and truly over him and much the wiser. I'll never fall for that type of guy again.'

Her vehemence must've struck a chord as he turned to look at her. 'What type is that?'

'Charming, demanding, successful, mega-wealthy.'

'Funny, you could've just described me,' he said, staring directly into her eyes.

'If the shoe fits.'

She shrugged, tried to make it sound light-hearted but her words sounded mean even to her own ears and he visibly recoiled.

'Sorry. There are loads of differences between you and Julian.'

Reaching out, she placed a comforting hand on his shoulder. Big mistake. He covered it with his own hand, caressing her with his thumb.

'Let's hope this is just one of them,' he muttered as he pulled her towards him.

His lips covered hers in an explosion of searing heat. Lips and tongues fused, melding together in endless, unquenchable hunger.

Long, hot kisses that deepened and delved until she couldn't breathe.

Soft, moist, seductive kisses that stole her heart along with her breath.

She knew this was crazy, knew it would change their working relationship, but every glance, every touch, every conversation had been leading to this point and she had no intention of letting him back down now.

Besides, she couldn't think with his hands everywhere, tugging at the shirt tucked into her waistband, stroking her back, winding through her tangled hair.

How could she have dared to compare this man with Julian? They were nothing alike; Rhys had the power to undo her completely and she'd never given herself to Julian in that way, ever.

She could see that now, see it all so clearly. Falling in love with a dream, a dream of the perfect romance rather than falling for the man. Silly, naïve, but then, considering her closeted upbringing, maybe she wasn't completely at fault. Brought up in the lap of luxury, taught to expect the best in everything, she hadn't doubted Julian and his dazzling image.

Thankfully she'd wised up, had her eyes opened in the worst possible way. Now, under the expert tutelage of Rhys with his sensual, searing kisses and his soothing hands, she could banish memories of her ex once and for all.

She gasped as he unhooked her bra and cupped her breasts in both hands, stroking her hardened nipples, the rigid peaks begging for his touch, and as he nibbled a trail from her mouth to her breast she melted, her bones liquefying.

Leaning back, she exposed her breasts to his feasting mouth as he licked and teased the aching nub on one breast while slowly circling his thumb on the other.

Electrifying shocks shot through her, making her damp with need.

She wanted him. Inside her. Now.

She'd never felt like this. Sex had been fun but rather repetitive, at times unfulfilling. Never had she experienced the heat that raced through her body at Rhys's touch, threatening to spontaneously combust her on the spot. Rhys and his wondrous tongue were driving her to the brink of losing control and she lapped up every glorious sensation.

Her hands took on a life of their own as she reached for him, ripping his shirt open as she'd yearned to do as soon as she laid eyes on it. Each button gave a satisfying pop as finally she encountered a delectable wall of naked skin.

Her hands went wild, sliding across his chest and downwards to the ridges of abdominal muscle, exploring every smooth contour.

'You're so hot,' she murmured, her hands stilling as they reached his belt, her fingertips skating around his waist, itching to delve deeper.

His hooded gaze followed the route her fingertips took, his body stilling when she hovered over his fly.

Her heart clamoured, filling her ears with a dull roar as he reached out, covered her hand with his and pressed it against the thick bulge.

'Go ahead, I'm all yours.'

She gasped as his erection leapt beneath her palm, large and hard and begging for attention.

Tentatively at first, she traced its outline, empowered by his ragged breathing, his low moans, his pelvis arching into her hand.

'Jade…'

Her name tumbled from his lips, half plea, half groan and, emboldened, she slid the long strap of leather through the belt buckle, taking it slow, real slow.

'You're killing me,' he said through gritted teeth, though his heavy passion-glazed stare told her he was enjoying her prolonging the anticipation as much as she was.

Deliberately grazing her knuckles against his erection, she smiled, a purely wicked smile solely for him. 'That's not my intention.'

She snapped the top button on his jeans. 'I want you—' she grabbed the zipper and tugged it down inch by torturous inch '—very much—' she inveigled her hands beneath the waistband

and tugged down, stripping the jeans down his long legs where he shucked out of them '—alive.'

All the air whooshed out of her lungs at the sight of him reclining on the plush rug in front of the fire, the flames dancing across his incredible body, wearing nothing but black briefs and a hedonistic smile.

'You were saying?'

She'd been speaking? Not any more. She'd passed the point of coherent speech about two seconds ago when she'd caught her first glimpse of his gloriously naked body.

Almost.

'I was saying I want you alive.' With trembling hands, she slid her fingers into the top of his briefs. 'For this.'

Her breath along with her fingers snagged as she peeled his briefs off, her hands trembling as his erection jutted towards her, thick and long and proud.

'Oh, my…'

'You okay?'

Speechless, she nodded, her eyes fixed on exactly how okay she was.

'Come here.'

She didn't have to be asked twice, eager to get naked alongside him, desperate to feel him inside her.

In a frantic rush of tugging hands and tearing cotton, her clothes joined his on the floor, his hands caressing her curves, delving into dips and honing in on the one area about to detonate.

'Oh, yeah, like that,' she panted, taking an embarrassingly short time to twist and writhe and beg for release. A release that came moments after he sheathed himself and slid into her with one, smooth thrust.

As he drove into her the friction of their sweat-slicked bodies caused her to climax again, riding crest after crest of exquisite spasms, crying out his name, urging him to join her.

He did with an almighty roar, a deep, guttural sound that made her feel all woman and then some.

She clasped him to her, savouring their intimate bond, not willing to break it just yet.

For she knew what would happen then.

Questions, recriminations, and this felt too damn good to waste time pondering regrets.

Besides, the night was young.

They'd only just started on dessert.

CHAPTER TWELVE

Rhys watched Jade sleep, not caring about his dead arm as her head lay snuggled in the crook of it.

Beautiful awake, she was transcendental asleep, her long eyelashes fanning shadows across her smooth cheeks, her skin flushed from their third sex-capade, her lips curved into a small, satisfied smile.

But it wasn't her beauty tugging at him as much as her generosity as a lover, her unselfish focus on giving him pleasure, her unbridled enthusiasm.

Jeez, had he misjudged her. Uptight, society princess couldn't be further from the truth. Warm, passionate woman with a real zest for life would be more apt. And that was what scared him.

He could handle keeping her at arm's length while he viewed her as remote, untouchable, a fickle woman playing at something new for a while. But with every confidence revealed, with every heart-to-heart chat, with every intimate touch over the last few hours, she'd stripped away every logical, sane reason he should maintain his distance.

A dull ache settled in his chest, a persistent, nagging twinge he remembered too well.

He'd never forget the gut-wrenching agony of hearing the brother he adored had died, the never-ending days, months, where he slowly withdrew into himself until there was nothing left but to run. Run as fast and far as he could get from anything resembling emotional ties.

While he'd built bridges with Callum over the last few years, they were still a long way from being close friends as many brothers were and it suited him just fine.

Being close involved sharing confidences, sharing dreams, and he had a feeling his newly awakened starry-eyed brother wouldn't understand the relentless, driving need for him to bolt from anything remotely resembling emotion.

He'd never revealed the depth of his involvement with Claudia to Callum, had known his brother would see right through him: that he blamed himself for her death and would shoulder that guilt for the rest of his life, exactly how Callum had done following Archie's death.

He now understood why Callum had focused one hundred per cent on work after Archie's death; for being so absorbed in business, so driven to succeed, so hell-bent on success at the cost of everything else, allowed you to forget.

He'd done the same thing after Claudia died, throwing himself into building Wild Thing, pretending to relish the CEO role behind a desk, not returning here.

It had helped for a time, distance from where it had happened allowing him to compartmentalise that part of his life and lock it away. Yet being back here didn't stir up those memories half as much as what he'd done with Jade last night.

It wasn't the sex itself but the implied intimacy, the depth of feeling he'd glimpsed in her eyes when he'd been inside her that dredged up part of him best left forgotten, the part of him that dared to feel.

It terrified him. *Feeling.* He'd loved Archie unreservedly and the pain of his death had shattered him, irrevocably setting him on a life path he still couldn't veer from. Then Claudia had died, another person he'd risked caring about, cementing what he already knew: being emotionally invested led to eventual grief.

He couldn't bear going through any of that again: loving, losing, and that was exactly what would happen if he was foolish enough to let Jade into his heart.

Jade stirred, wriggled closer, turning her face to bury it into his chest, and the very organ he'd do anything to protect lurched.

Now he had the added guilt of this.

Far from getting her out of his system, sex with Jade had only served to make him crave her more and he could see the whole scenario of the next few months playing out before his eyes.

Sensational sex, more talks, growing increasingly attached, which would only serve to make him pull back, hurting her in the process.

Just as he'd hurt Claudia doing the same thing; sadly for her, his inherent inability to grow emotionally attached had been fatal.

Squeezing his eyes shut, he tried to block out the feel of Jade snuggled close, tried to erase the image of the two of them doing this on a nightly basis for the rest of her time here.

Most of all, he tried to eradicate the awful, sinking feeling that in such a short time she'd crashed through every preconceived notion he'd ever had and made him truly feel for the first time in for ever.

Jade awoke to the pounding of an axe.

Thud…thud…thud…

She didn't know whether the sound was real or some misplaced fantasy where Rhys had assumed the starring role of lumberjack.

Stretching, she pried open one eye, then the other, surprised to see sun streaming through her bedroom windows. She hadn't slept in once since she'd arrived here, preferring to wake at dawn and make the most of every second of every day.

Something she'd certainly done last night and then some! Smiling like a well-satisfied woman, she rolled out of bed, wrapping the sheet around her as she padded across to the window.

A small part of her had hoped she'd wake to find Rhys cuddled up next to her, but she'd given up on believing in fairy tales around the time she'd learned the truth about her parents' marriage and Julian's cheating.

Rhys hadn't made any promises last night. What they'd done was simple: indulge a mutual attraction that had been building towards consummation for a while now.

Sex. Nothing more, nothing less.

But the moment she caught sight of him, tan T-shirt wet and clinging to his broad chest, swinging an axe like a man possessed, the *flump* of her heart made a mockery of her 'just sex' declaration.

Since when had she ever had *just sex* anyway?

With a sigh she clutched the sheet tighter and rested her forehead against the glass, her body tingling with remembrance as she watched his muscles bunch and shift and flex across his chest, his torso, his arms, those strong, sure hands gripping the axe as they'd gripped her hips as he'd plunged into her again and again…

Straightening, she rubbed at the huge condensation patch on the window from her heavy breathing, only to find Rhys looking up at her.

He must've mistaken her cleaning action for a wave and now he'd know she'd been perving on him. So much for morning-after subtlety.

Managing a sheepish grin, she waved, properly this time, the bubble of happiness cocooning her bursting with a resounding pop as he merely inclined his head and resumed the axe-swinging.

Oh-oh. That nod didn't look like the nod of a guy who'd had a fabulous night and wanted a repeat performance. That nod looked like the nod of a guy slamming the barriers back into place. A nod of regret, a nod of distance, a nod of the one-night stand.

Calling him a rather choice name under her breath, she trudged towards the bathroom, trailing the sheet forlornly behind her.

Today should've been a day for coy smiles and subtle flirting. From that aloof nod, today would be a day for tiptoeing around a hard-headed guy without a clue.

Stepping into the bathroom, she caught a glimpse of herself in the mirror and dropped the sheet in shock. Her eyes were shadowed, her lips swollen from long, slow kisses that lasted all night long, her skin a faint pink from the delicious abrading of his stubble.

She looked like a woman who'd been thoroughly satisfied. Repeatedly.

She also looked like a woman in no shape to face a recalcitrant guy hell-bent on doing some serious back-pedalling.

And that hurt, a lot.

No matter how much she could delude herself into believing last night was just about sex, she knew the truth. She would never have slept with him if she didn't care.

That made his rejection this morning all the harder to bear.

She rubbed her stomach as it rebelled at the thought of walking downstairs and facing him for the first time since he'd rocked her world. Sitting across from him at the dining table, sharing breakfast, small talk, platitudes, all the while determinedly ignoring the persistent ache in her heart that he didn't want to acknowledge what they'd shared last night.

Bracing her hands on the vanity, she peered into the mirror, tilting her head from side to side.

She was too easy to read, needed to hide her morning-after jitters with a good trowelling of make-up. Though how she'd hide the wounded expression in her eyes... With a groan, she swivelled away and padded across the marble tiles to the shower.

She needed an action plan: hot bracing shower, blow-dried hair, make-up to hide a multitude of sins and businesslike outfit.

Presenting a professional front would surely help quell the nerves making her belly tumble?

Only one way to find out.

With a final swing Rhys buried the axe in the trunk so deeply he'd need the guys to help him pry it out.

Swiping the sweat off his forehead, he risked a quick glance at the window where he'd spied Jade. Thankfully, she'd gone, but that didn't ease the guilt lodged like a wood chip in his skin.

Even from a distance, he'd seen the glow on her face, the tentative smile, the half wave. And what had he done? Acted like a jerk.

Chopping wood was his way of working off steam, the relentless, monotonous job the perfect thinking time. Unfortunately, no matter how many logs he'd chopped this morning, he couldn't forget last night and how she'd made him feel.

Like a guy who could get used to having her around for as long as she stayed.

He could see how the next few months would pan out: sharing the giant hot tub together, bumping hips as they stood side by side in the kitchen whipping up decadent suppers, lying in front of the fire, sated, like last night.

He could see it all so clearly yet when he'd lain in bed this morning, wide awake while she dreamed, a tiny hint of a satisfied smile curling the corners of her mouth, something about seeing her so vulnerable had got to him.

He'd told her he didn't do relationships and she'd fired it right back at him. Made sense after what she'd been through. As long as she meant it maybe they had a shot at having some fun while she was here, nothing too deep.

Then she'd woken, looked up at him with blatant tenderness, her eyes crinkled with sleep yet so easy to read, filled with an emotion that scared the hell out of him, and he'd known in an instant that no words could put boundaries around what was happening here.

She was already in too deep.

No matter how much he liked her, how much he'd love to indulge their mutual passion over the next few months while she was here, he knew the closer they grew, the harder it would be on her in the end.

He couldn't do that to her.

After what she'd been through, she deserved better. Better than him and what he could offer.

With a growl, he ripped off his T-shirt, welcoming the frosty bite of frigid air against his heated skin.

He couldn't stay out here all day. He'd have to face her eventually. Heading for the house and a hot shower, he thought, *No time like the present.*

As Jade entered the kitchen she didn't know what smelled more delicious: the mouth-watering aroma of sizzling bacon or the tempting scent of freshly showered male.

Determined to play this cool and perky, she peeked over Rhys's shoulder.

'Something smells good.'

He stiffened at her proximity, a disheartening reaction on a par with that distant nod.

'Take a seat, I'll dish up. You hungry?'

Yeah, but not for food.

When she didn't answer, he glanced over his shoulder and she quickly nodded before sitting at the enormous granite-topped breakfast bar.

'You must've worked up an appetite.'

The skillet in his hand paused in midair, the fried egg in danger of slipping back into the pan as she belatedly realised her comment could've referred to their sexual gymnastics last night as much as his lumberjack impersonation.

'Chopping all that wood.'

He nodded in response, plonked her egg alongside rashers of crispy bacon, a hash brown and wholegrain toast.

She could've let him off the hook. Instead, she toyed with her cutlery, glanced at him from beneath her lashes.

'Must've been hard work, what with you having an axe to grind.'

Sliding her plate in front of her, he scooted around the breakfast bar, preferring to keep a solid mass of marble between them. What did he think she was going to do—jump him?

'I needed some time to think. Chopping wood helps with that.'

'Right.'

With her stomach churning, she forked some egg into her mouth, made an effort to chew and swallow, when her appetite had taken a nosedive around the time he'd chosen to remain at arm's length.

'Jade, I—'

'What—?'

They laughed.

'Ladies first,' he said, looking relieved he wouldn't have to broach their awkwardness first.

'What were you thinking about?'

Rather than toying with her food, she laid her fork on the plate, pushed it away. The tiny mouthful of egg she'd managed to eat sat undigested in her gut, uncomfortable.

To his credit, he didn't look away.

'Setting the record straight.'

The egg curdled further.

'About?'

'Us. Last night.'

If he gave her the 'it's not you, it's me' line, she'd clobber him over the head with the still-hot frying pan.

Pre-empting him, she held up a finger. 'Let me guess. While it was fabulous, you don't want a repeat. Because we work together. Because we practically live together. Because you don't want a relationship. Yada, yada, yada.'

The corners of his mouth lifted, admiration glimmering in his eyes.

She didn't want his admiration, damn it, she wanted his l… What? Love? Uh-uh. Way too complicated. Way too much. Way too soon.

But as she sat across from him in this glorious kitchen with its yawning granite bench-tops and pristine stainless-steel appliances and state-of-the-art fridge, the pale morning sun filtering through the wide windows and bathing him in an incandescent glow, she knew that all the protests in the world couldn't deny it.

She might have fallen in love with her boss.

Inwardly cringing, she clasped her hands together in her lap to stop from strangling herself.

'Isn't that the spiel you were going to give me?'

He shook his head. 'No spiel. I just wanted to clear the air.'

'Didn't know it was murky to begin with.'

She wouldn't give an inch, wouldn't let him see how his inevitable pulling-away speech hurt.

Muttering a curse, he rubbed his jaw, drawing her attention to it and the telltale stubble there. She'd never seen him anything but groomed and clean-shaven, and the sight of that stubble proved what she already knew.

He'd been so wound up about last night he'd bolted for his axe marathon without taking the time to shave.

Sighing, she slammed her palms on the bench-top, leaned forward.

'Give it to me straight. No bull.'

His eyes widened a fraction before he nodded. 'You want it straight? Fine. What happened last night can't happen again.'

Tilting her chin up, she eyeballed him. 'Why?'

'Because it's complicated.'

'You sure? From where I was, the sex was—'

'I'm not talking about that and you damn well know it.'

She did, but she enjoyed having him on the back foot and, for some perverse, masochistic reason, needed to hear him articulate exactly what was going on.

'So explain this complication to me.'

He pushed off the bench-top, swung around to stare out of the window, before turning back to face her, his expression shuttered.

'I don't do relationships.'

'Neither do I.'

'You were engaged, for God's sake!'

'Exactly why I'm not heading down that track again.' She rolled her eyes. 'Haven't we already established all this?'

Pinching the bridge of his nose, he took a few moments to come up with another offensive. *Bring it on, Ranger.*

'Look, this will sound lame, but I don't do the sleeping-together-living-together thing. Let's just leave it at that.'

'Let's not.'

She'd asked for no bull. All she'd got was a truckload of the stuff, freshly dumped.

His mouth thinned in rebellion. So he was stubborn? Big deal. She could out-stubborn him and then some.

Stalking around the bench, she stood toe to toe with him, his freshly showered scent putting a serious dent in her full head of steam.

Exhaling in an exasperated huff, she jabbed him in the chest. 'What happened last night was a result of us dancing around each other for ages. We're attracted to each other. We're consenting adults—what's the big deal?'

'The big deal is—'

'Rhetorical question. Let me finish.'

Another jab, harder this time, to ram her point home. 'The harassment thing is moot. Mutual all the way. No expectations either side, so how hard can this be?'

A plethora of emotions flickered across his face, from hope to regret, obstinacy to optimism, before he finally settled for resignation.

'You ever had a one-night stand?'

Confused, she shook her head. 'No.'

'Consider last night your first.'

Pain slashed through her, sharp, brutal, her hand falling use-lessly to her side as she stepped back, anxious to put as much space between them as possible.

He stood there like a statue carved from stone, just as rigid, just as cold.

Swallowing the lump welling in her throat, she silently prayed her voice remained steady.

'Guess my judgement's way off again.'

Her gaze flicked over him, scathing, derisive. 'Never would've picked you for a bastard too.'

Turning on her heel, she fled without a backward glance.

CHAPTER THIRTEEN

'Where's Jade?'

Trying not to wince at Cody's question as they unloaded supplies, Rhys grunted as he hoisted a particularly heavy box.

'She's not feeling well.'

Not that he actually knew, considering she hadn't spoken to him since their confrontation that morning.

He could barely stomach what he'd done, what he'd said to push her away. Yet despite his roiling gut and hideous guilt, he knew it was ultimately for the best.

Short-term pain for long-term gain. That was what he'd been telling himself all day and he'd better stick to it before he marched into the east wing and broke down her door to grovel on his knees and apologise.

She'd lumped him in with her bastard of an ex. The way he'd behaved he deserved it, but it still hurt like the devil.

Cody paused mid-lift. 'She's sick? That's unusual. Fit as a Mallee bull, she keeps telling me, whatever a Mallee bull is.'

'Drop it.'

Cursing his abrupt response and the curiosity it was sure to garner, he turned his back on Cody.

'You two have a lovers' tiff?'

Rhys swung around too quickly, dropping the box he carried onto his big toe and letting rip a justifiable curse, more to do with the day he'd had rather than his throbbing toe.

Cody smirked. 'Guess I have my answer right there.'

'Shut the hell up.'

Rhys perched on a nearby log and flexed his foot, seething that he'd let himself get sucked into this conversation. If he'd played it cool, Cody wouldn't have pushed.

'You're grumpier than usual. Jade is holed up in her room. Something must've happened.'

Yeah, something had happened all right, a big something, where he'd had the most amazing sex of his life, made a real connection with a woman, only to deliberately alienate her completely in some warped notion that he'd be saving her from hurt in the long run.

Gingerly testing his foot on terra firma, he glared at Cody. 'We had a falling out, nothing major.'

Cody shook his head. 'Man, you two are a bonfire just waiting to happen. Enough kindling, the right conditions, set a match and, whoosh, combustion.'

He couldn't have summed it up better himself. They combusted all right, the memory of hot, deep kisses and plunging into her tight heat replaying across his mind no matter how hard he tried to turn the erotic images off.

'This isn't funny. Jade's a great worker. I'd hate to lose her this early in her contract.'

'She won't bail. Jade's a fighter.'

Yeah, he'd got a glimpse of that too this morning.

'Which begs the question, if you two aren't talking, how are things meant to run smoothly around here?'

'We'll manage.'

Satisfied his foot could take full weight, Rhys started stacking some of the smaller boxes, ignoring his increasingly annoying voice of reason that insisted he'd have to grovel before Jade would even look his way, let alone work alongside him.

Casting him a sly glance, Cody slung him a few boxes to add to the stack. 'Why don't you two get together, get it out of your systems?'

In an instant, memories swamped him: the soft, panting noises she made as he thrust inside her, her uninhibited enthusiasm to explore him as thoroughly as he'd explored her, the snug way she fitted into him, curved into his side all night…

He'd tried to get her out of his system and it had blown up in his face.

He now craved her more than ever.

'Work!'

He'd known Cody a long time, liked the guy as a friend as well as a trusted employee, but taking advice on his love life wasn't on the agenda.

'Whatever you say, boss.'

Smart guy, he knew when to back off.

As they worked in silence he almost wished Cody would start annoying him again. All this quiet left him to his thoughts and, no matter how he looked at it, he knew he'd have to do something to fix things with Jade.

In the ideal world, the situation was tailor-made for him. He'd head back to Vancouver in a few months, Jade back to Australia. Short term. No commitment. No lasting promises. No ties.

But he knew it was a lie. Jade wasn't as footloose and fancy-free as she liked to portray. She'd been engaged and women who were willing to walk down the aisle secretly harboured dreams of grand romance and emotional involvement.

He didn't need the complication.

He didn't need her.

As he glanced towards the east wing, at her bedroom window where he'd seen her staring longingly at him less than ten hours earlier, the serious twinge in his chest made a mockery of his denials.

Jade welcomed Cody's and Jack's return with open arms. After an afternoon of hiding out—alternating between stomping and cursing and crying—she was ready for battle.

Not that she planned on fighting with Rhys. Oh, no, she had a much better plan. Focus on work, be civil and when in doubt, ignore. Very mature, very civilised.

'Gawd, you look awful.'

She winced as Cody elbowed Jack in the ribs. 'You can't say that to a lady, you baboon.'

Jack glanced from Cody to her, confused. 'Sorry, Jade. Just

thought you'd like to know. Your eyes look real puffy. Did something sting you?'

She suppressed laughter. Yeah, Rhys's tongue had aimed a few barbs her way.

'Must've been a stray wood chip. Rhys was chopping earlier— a chip probably flew up.'

'In both eyes?' Jack muttered as Cody elbowed him again.

'Help me get this stuff packed away, you big oaf.' Cody winked at Jade as he pushed Jack towards the supplies and she smiled her thanks.

'Well, this place looks like a hive of activity.'

She stiffened at the sound of Rhys's deep voice behind her, every rebellious cell in her body leaping to attention. Her libido shouldn't twang like this, not after what he'd said, but it looked as if her body had missed the chill-out memo her mind had dictated earlier.

Mustering her best blasé expression, the one her mum used to snub people beneath her to great effect, she turned towards him.

'We're sorting supplies. Want to help?'

She expected him to bolt but, then again, when did he ever do anything she expected?

'Sure.'

'We'll offload the rest of the stuff. Jack, come help.'

Intuitive, Cody raised an eyebrow and she nodded, grateful for the time alone with Rhys. If they were to continuing working together, she had a few things to say.

'Need a hand?'

Of course Rhys wanted to help the boys. He must've caught a glimpse of the smoke pouring out of her ears.

'We've got it covered, boss. You stay and help Jade.'

Giving her a thumbs-up sign behind Rhys's back, Cody headed off, leaving her with a man who looked decidedly uncomfortable. Maybe the guy had a conscience after all.

'You seem to have everything under control. Maybe I'll start dinner—'

'Stay.'

To her amazement, a faint pink stained his cheeks. Could her suave, rugged boss be blushing? Could he actually have a heart?

Squaring her shoulders, she eyeballed him. 'I owe you an apology.'

His eyebrows shot up, his shocked expression almost comical.

'Calling my boss a bastard doesn't exactly hold me in good stead for employee of the year, so I'm sorry.'

'I should be the one apologising.'

Jamming his hands into the back pockets of his jeans, he rolled back on the balls of his feet, edgy and awkward.

'I acted like a jerk.'

And then some, but this wasn't about rehashing what they'd said. It was about establishing a working relationship so she could get through the rest of her tenure without falling apart and running back to Sydney with her dreams of being a biologist in tatters.

'At least we both know where we stand.'

The awkward silence lengthened and she glanced away, uncomfortable beneath his piercing stare. He looked at her as if he wanted to say more, regret evident in the down-turning of his mouth, in his morose expression.

Sadly, there was nothing more to say.

She was a complication he didn't want; he was a complication she didn't need.

Frowning, he said, 'This is—'

'How it's going to be 'til my contract runs out.'

Pointing at the next box to be shifted, she squatted to get a good grip. 'Give me a hand?'

With a terse nod, he did just that.

They worked in silence until Cody and Jack returned, and as she joined in the boys' usual ribbing she couldn't help but mourn the loss of the closeness she'd developed with Rhys.

They'd talked, they'd laughed, they'd screwed it all up by having sex.

As he bent to hoist the last few boxes she struggled to keep her gaze off his butt—and lost—one thought echoing through her head.

What a damn shame.

As Jade dragged the last of the heavy branches out of the forest and into a small clearing she took one look at Rhys standing like a sentinel over the towering pile of wood offcuts and wanted to bolt back into the welcome darkness of the trees.

Swinging an axe to fell saplings, wielding a machete to trim branches, stacking wood, stripping back and repainting canoes she could handle—though her aching, calloused hands would probably argue the point—but another second under his cool indifference would make her take an axe to him.

It had been a month, four long, excruciatingly long, weeks, where she'd done her best to act professional, tackling every task with unbridled enthusiasm, determined to show him that what had happened between them didn't affect her in the slightest.

At first she'd thought his pushing her to take on more tasks, more responsibility, was another test, seeing how far she'd go before cracking. But he wasn't unfair in his demands, just bossy and superior, exactly how he'd been at the start when he'd set that challenge.

This time he was using work as a reinforcement of their relationship. Him, boss; her, employee.

She should be glad. Focusing on doing a good job and showing him she was more than up for any task he set kept her mind off that one, incredible night they'd shared, and what they could have again if he weren't so pig-headed.

Though her sweeter-than-honey employee-of-the-month routine was wearing him down. She could tell. The harder she strove without protesting, the tenser he became. And she'd caught him checking her out. Several times, which only served to spike her latent anger.

For she was angry, furious in fact, that they'd had one wonderful night together and could have more if he weren't so darn stubborn. He'd hurt her and she'd coped by throwing herself into work, but regret that he'd broken off their fledgling relationship before they'd given it a chance still gnawed, urging her to do something about it.

She wouldn't have got this far—leaving her cushy life behind, doggedly pursuing her dream, determined to ultimately make it as a biologist—if she were content to sit back and let things happen. She liked her newfound independence, liked being in control of her own destiny, which made this situation even more untenable.

What was the point of mincing words and tiptoeing around each other in a taut working relationship when they could be relaxed, easy-going, enjoying each other's company socially and professionally? *And physically*, though she wouldn't go there now, not when his reticence to acknowledge the sparks between them had her so close to breaking point that one more itty-bitty confrontation and she'd snap like the twigs on the kindling pile.

Surely she wasn't the only edgy one, yet there he stood, clutching his clipboard, master of his domain, cool, imperturbable, infuriating.

What she wouldn't give to shake him up a little, test his mettle, see if work-focused Ranger was as unflappable as he portrayed.

It came to her in that second.

She'd done the right thing over the last month, being the model employee, subduing her hurt at his rejection, agreeing to the emotionless terms he'd set. And what had it got her? His admiration for her job skills and little else. Time to change the status quo. Up the ante. He might have set the boundaries for their relationship, but that didn't mean she couldn't push them, right?

Hoisting the heavy branch onto her shoulder for extra effect, she marched across the clearing and dumped it on top of the stack she'd already collected.

'That's the last of them. What's next?'

He didn't glance up from his clipboard, his frown clear indication her jaunty tone pained him as much as her accomplishing another task in record time.

'Take a breather.'

'I'd rather keep going. Build up my stamina.'

He glanced up, his frown intensifying, while something un-fathomable shifted behind those ice-blue eyes.

'You've done enough for today. Take the afternoon off.'

'Maybe Cody and Jack need a hand? Clearing undergrowth from the picnic area is a huge job. I'm sure they'd like some help—'

'You need a break. Take it.'

He swung away, but not before she'd seen guilt streak across his face. So the guy had a heart, buried deep beneath layers of self-imposed guilt and macho bravado.

She could do as he said, take the easy option. But their monthly supply run was coming up fast and this time it was their turn to head into Skagway. Things were tense enough now; no way could she put up with any more.

'I don't need a break. I need—'

You. One little word, so simple yet so complex.

He swung back to face her, his expression wary.

Not willing to push that far yet, she pretended to examine her blistered hands.

'I need a manicure, badly.'

His relief was comical. 'Can't help you there.'

Spurred by a little mischievous imp residing in her brain, she stepped closer, rolled her shoulders.

'Maybe another of those massages you're so good at?'

Heat flared in his eyes before he damped it with a deliberate blink.

'No.'

'Pity, because I've got a really tight spot right about here.'

She lifted one shoulder before stretching it back, biting back a triumphant laugh when his gaze strayed to her breasts stretched against the cool wool of her crimson jumper.

'And here.'

Turning around, she pointed to her lower back, knowing where his gaze would end up—about a foot lower.

'Don't push me, Jade.'

His gravelly voice sent a shiver of yearning through her as she slowly turned back to face him, grateful it had come to this.

'Like how you've pushed me?'

'That's different. It's work,' he ground out, flinging the clipboard away and thrusting his hands into his pockets.

Taking a step, another, she got right up close, close enough for her sensory receptors to hit overload the minute she inhaled his addictive outdoorsy scent.

'Is it?'

'Yes, damn it.'

His rebuke lost some of its force when she smiled, refusing to give an inch.

He took a step back, she took a step forward, spurred by the need to confront him and his crazy ideas of ignoring this thing between them.

'Here's what I think.' She laid her palm against his chest. 'I think you're hoping I'll crack. The harder you push me, you think the angrier I'll get. Who knows—maybe you want me to quit?'

Her palm slid upward, rested over his heart, to show him she meant business. 'Well, here's a news flash for you. I'm made of sterner stuff than that.'

Tilting her head up, she met his steely gaze unflinchingly. 'I can handle anything you care to dish out and more, Ranger.'

He didn't move, every muscle rigid, the hard angles of his face highlighted by the wan sunlight dappling the clearing.

She had no idea how long they stood there, toe to toe, each unwilling to back down, the silence amplifying every breath frosting the air between them.

Then a shift, a small one, as he angled his body towards her rather than stepping away, the corners of his mouth easing into a smile that snatched her breath and made her crave him more than ever.

'Maybe it's time to ditch the Princess tag?' He gestured at the wood pile. 'Perhaps Wonder Woman fits better these days?'

She chuckled, buoyed by his backhanded compliment.

'See this?' She touched his mouth, briefly traced his smile, before dropping her hand. 'I want to see more of that in Skagway. Lose the angst. It's not working.'

To his credit, he didn't play dumb. 'Focusing on business is easier than thinking about us.'

She snapped her fingers. 'Well, golly, Ranger, and here I was, unaware there was even an us.'

'Bit late for coyness.'

Patting his big, broad chest, she glanced up from beneath her lashes. 'I'm not the one playing hard to get.'

He laughed outright at that and for a long, exquisite moment, when his gaze drifted to her lips, she thought he might kiss her.

'Nothing has essentially changed. We still can't be together.'

'So you keep saying,' she muttered, annoyed that the faux closeness of the last few moments, the lovely flirting, the easing of residual tension only to be replaced by sexual tension, had vanished.

This time, when he stepped away, she knew the spell had broken. 'Did the boys mention the accommodation situation in Skagway?'

'About hotels booked out by the fishing convention? Yeah, they told me.'

He hesitated, and she didn't make it easier for him, knowing the source of his unease. 'And you're okay with staying at my condo?'

'I'm okay if you are.'

She hadn't been, not at the start. When Cody had told her she'd pretended to nod and act all businesslike, saving her hissy fit for back in her room. The way Rhys had treated her the last month she'd rather sleep buck naked in an igloo than share a condo with him, until reality hit.

This supply trip was all business; Rhys wanted to pretend all they had between them was business. Let them see how long Ranger lasted in business mode when they had to be in each other's faces for a weekend.

'Don't worry, I'm immune to you now. Your virtue's safe.'

In a flash he'd captured her chin, brushing his thumb with tantalising, deliberate thoroughness across her bottom lip.

'Immune, huh?'

He swooped in for a kiss, a quick, hard, prove-a-point meshing of lips before he broke it off, picked up his clipboard and strode away without looking back.

Lucky for her, for her knees shook so hard she plopped onto the nearest log and ended up dislodging her neat woodpile and sending the lot scattering.

Great. Looked as if her work efforts were in the same state as her resolve.

In tatters.

Dumping his backpack on the rocky shore, Rhys scanned the forest edge for Jade. She should've been here by now. Maybe she'd backed out of the supply trip? After their confrontation yesterday, he could live in hope.

One month had passed since they'd slept together.

Four long weeks.

Twenty-eight excruciatingly long days.

He'd tried the polite, cool, distant approach, he'd tried the reserved approach, he'd tried the pushy boss approach, yet Jade acted the same, treating him with respect underlined by wry amusement. As if she was waiting for him to snap and change his mind about their *situation*.

He should be happy. She was the model employee: dedicated, driven, enthusiastic. When the tourists filled out feedback forms at the end of a day in the wilderness, her name popped up constantly, carving him a regular dose of humble pie.

Initially, he'd expected her to fail spectacularly out here, had half expected to send her back on the first JetCat out of here. But she'd surpassed his wildest expectations.

And his wildest fantasies.

He groaned, swiped a hand over his face. It did little to wipe the constant X-rated flick playing in his head, the one that remembered every torturous detail of their one staggering night together.

Seeing her every day over the last month yet being unable to touch had been pure torture. He'd wanted it this way, didn't need the complication. But what if trying to hold her at bay made things worse rather than better?

Damn, he needed her. It had moved past wanting a long time ago. If it had been that easy, having sex would've scratched that itch and he could've moved on. Instead, he couldn't eat, couldn't sleep, without constantly thinking about her, wishing for something he could never risk having.

Then she had to go and push him yesterday, baiting him, teasing him to get a response and, hot damn, he'd given it to her. He'd already been hanging on to his shredded self-control by a thread and after four long, tense weeks her deliberate goading had got to him. He'd snapped.

That kiss shouldn't have happened. Though he guessed he should be grateful he'd settled for a brief kiss when he'd wanted so much more.

'Ready to go?'

He blinked as she strode towards him, all long denim-clad legs and tight red jumper highlighting curves that made his palms itch to run all over them.

'Sure.'

He looked away, out over the water, needing to focus on something else before she read the desperate yearning in his eyes. 'JetCat should be here in a minute.'

'No worries.'

She dumped her backpack next to his, bent to pick up a rock, and skipped it across the water.

'Where'd you learn to do that?'

'My dad.'

Her wary tone didn't invite further questions but he'd already damaged their relationship beyond repair. What was one more foot in mouth?

'Have you spoken to your folks since you got here?'

'Hell, no!'

She stood, dusted off her hands—of the rock or symbolic of washing her hands of her folks? 'Besides, I bet they're too busy traipsing around the world to even notice I'm gone.'

Something in her tone alerted him to a deep, dark hurt and

before he could second-guess himself he placed a hand on her shoulder. To his relief, she didn't shrug him off.

'You coming here was about them too, wasn't it?'

She chewed on her bottom lip, worrying it with her teeth, and he clamped down on the urge to trace its fullness with his fingertip.

Squeezing her shoulder, his hand dropped, but he didn't back away, standing close, there if she needed him.

With a resigned sigh, she glanced up and what he saw in her eyes punched him in the gut: disillusionment.

'What did they do?'

Apart from her dad pulling strings to get her this job, interfering, when he had a suspicion she'd throw a fit if she ever found out.

As if she was coming to a personal decision, her shoulders sagged, some of the tension draining out of her.

'I saw my dad with another woman. I told my mum. Know what she said?'

He shook his head, though he could guess. His parents moved in the same circles as hers, would happily shove any scandal under the priceless Aubusson rug rather than taint the perfect image.

'That I was naïve. Women in *our* position should expect things like this to happen, should turn a blind eye.'

Her mouth contorted. 'Men have *urges*, apparently, *it has nothing to do with the family* and *I'd do well to remember that for my own marriage*.'

He swore, guessing what came next.

'Like I'd ever put up with crap like that.'

Her hands fisted, her defeated posture snapping upright. 'So I confronted Julian, asked him if he'd ever play away on me, expecting him to say, "no way, honey, you're my one and only true love".'

She grimaced, one fisted hand banging against her leg. 'Know what happened? He looked guilty as sin, tried to bluster his way out of it.'

She swung away, her gaze focused on the incoming JetCat.

'Turns out dear old Julian had already done the dirty on me and when I turned to my parents for support, those pillars of society who'd always doted on me in the past, they basically said suck it up.'

So that was why Fred had called in the favour, insisting Rhys hire his daughter: sheer, unmitigated guilt.

The truth hovered, ready to spill, but he clamped his lips shut on the words she didn't need to hear right now. They currently existed in a better place than the last month, their light exchange yesterday paving the way for an easier supply trip. Telling her about Fred's interference now would only serve to ruin the weekend and he'd be damned if he spent the next few days holed up in his condo with a silent, furious woman.

'You did the right thing in coming here.'

Swinging back to face him, she raised an eyebrow. 'Did I? Sometimes I wonder.'

She was referring to him and their relationship and the mess he'd made of it.

Mentally letting rip a string of curses he'd learned through several countries around the world, he searched for the right words to say, something comforting, not trite.

In the end, he settled for, 'You deserve so much better.'

Her bitter laugh raised his hackles. 'Julian or my parents?'

Thankfully, she left off, *Or you*?

'Both,' he muttered, hesitating a moment before slinging an arm around her waist, wanting to comfort her, willing his touch to convey the compassion words couldn't.

They stood there like that, watching the JetCat approach, and when her body finally relaxed and sagged against him, something terrifying twanged his heart.

Hard.

CHAPTER FOURTEEN

EXHAUSTED, Jade sank onto the edge of a huge king-size bed.

All her hard work over the last month, maintaining a business relationship, keeping emotional barriers in place, demolished in a few minutes standing on that rocky shore at Glacier Point.

Rhys had been so supportive, so understanding…and she'd blurted all that stuff about her family, initially horrified, until he'd held her.

It had hit her then, the reality of why she'd felt so betrayed by her parents' and Julian. She'd spent her entire life being cosseted, secure in her parents' love, their wealth, their lifestyle. Then Julian had come along and she'd coasted into the same life with him: money, prestige, status, safe from the harsher aspects of life, safe from everyday doubts that plagued most people, safe from insecurities. And they'd ripped that away from her when the ugly truths had surfaced.

So how come a guy she'd only known for a few weeks had the power to make her feel better about herself?

His simple words, *'you deserve better'*. After everything that had happened with her folks and Julian, she'd doubted her own judgement.

Had she deliberately seen their world through rose-tinted glasses, happy to only see the good stuff and ignore the bad? Had she missed signs along the way? Had she been so foolishly wrapped up in her cushy life she'd been oblivious to tensions around her?

After she'd initially learned the truth it had felt as if her whole world had crumbled around her, a fake world built on appearances and wealth and deception.

It wasn't only her judgement that had taken a serious hit: her self-confidence had suffered too. Yet in a brief moment of comfort Rhys had managed to salvage some of that confidence for her, had reinforced what she knew deep down: she *did* deserve better.

Pity he couldn't see 'better' had been standing right in front of her, hers for the taking if he weren't so darn righteous and pig-headed.

With a moan she fell back on the comfy bed, a plump hand-woven silk duvet cushioning her fall as she stared up at the steel beams criss-crossing the ceiling.

If Rhys's house at Glacier Point had impressed, his apartment here in Skagway blew her mind.

Luxury all the way, from the highly polished golden oak floorboards, modular chrome and black furniture, incredible bedrooms, spectacular views over Skagway and surrounding mountain ranges and a hot tub on the balcony that could give a girl with wavering defences some seriously sinful ideas.

'Settled in?'

She sat bolt upright, her traitorous heart instantly leaping at the imposing figure in the doorway, filling the space, making the bedroom stifling, almost airless, with him standing there staring at her.

She'd worked so hard over the last month, had been proud of her enforced immunity, but now her barriers lay in tatters, all her self-talk of the last twenty-eight days meant jack in the face of this guy and the power he had over her.

'Yeah, thanks, didn't have much to unpack.'

'Want to head into town and grab a bite to eat or are you too tired?'

She'd like nothing better than to take a long, hot bath then slide into bed on high-thread-count sheets, but maybe being surrounded by people in her current mood was better than being holed up here with him?

For there was nothing surer than her wanting to get close to him tonight. After what he'd said at Glacier Point, how he'd held her when she'd needed him to, she knew she couldn't hold out.

Simply, she'd never felt this way about any guy before. Her love for Julian, more a by-product of their life together and common goals, paled next to the depth of feeling for Rhys. And it terrified her.

She felt raw inside, open and vulnerable and yearning for more than he could give. But she had two options: coast along, not taking chances as she had her entire life, or continue exploring her reawakening self-confidence by opening herself up to the possibility of something wonderful, even if she knew it ultimately had to end.

'Sounds good. Give me ten minutes to take a shower, then I'm all yours.'

The moment the words tumbled out of her mouth she wished she could shove them right back. But rather than bolt, Rhys gave her a slow, heart-stopping smile.

'Lucky me,' he said, lingering for an exquisite moment longer before leaving her to fall back on the bed again, clutching her just-break-me-now heart.

Rhys paced the lounge room, his boots thudding on the floor-boards. Good. Perhaps the clomping of his boots would drown out the sounds of Jade taking a shower. He could just imagine her, soaping every inch of that tantalising body: stroking… scrubbing…rinsing…

Unable to stand, he dropped onto the sofa, leaned his head against the back of it. Doing the supply run with Jade and staying at his condo? Bad idea. After the agony of the last month, did he honestly think he could spend a weekend with her and come out unscathed at the other end?

No freaking way! But what else could he do? This weekend had been a way to make amends for his atrocious behaviour. He couldn't stand one more minute of her bravado, the hidden hurt occasionally visible when she'd glanced his way over the last month. She'd tried to hide it beneath a veneer of bravado, of gutsy professionalism, but it had broken his heart, staring into those chocolate-brown eyes and seeing that wounded expression lurking in the shadows.

Maybe, just maybe, she'd forgive him by the end of this weekend. If he didn't scare the living daylights out of her by looking at her as if he wanted to gobble her up, that was.

How could he have botched this so badly? He'd give anything to bury his face in her hair, to lavish her lush body with the attention it so richly deserved, to lick every delectable inch of her until she cried his name for more. He could've had that, could've been enjoying her company over the last month if he weren't so stubborn and focused on not needing anybody, ever.

'I'm ready.'

His head snapped forward so fast he got whiplash and he blinked, still lost in the erotic haze of his fantasy. Lucky him—his fantasy had come to life and was standing less than three feet away.

'Wow, you look great.'

She was nothing short of stunning, wearing a baby-pink cashmere twinset and a long denim skirt with knee-high black boots. The outfit clung to every curve and he swallowed, trying to ease the tightness in his throat, wishing he could do something about the tightness in his pants.

Though he wasn't a fan of make-up, he liked how she'd enhanced her eyes and lips, the shimmer of gloss making him want to lick every last drop from her lips.

'Thanks.'

She fidgeted with her hair, loose and mussed around her shoulders, her nerves matching his. They were acting like a couple of teens on their first date.

That was when it hit him.

In a way, this *was* their first date. They'd jumped from business colleagues to bedmates and back again, without a hint of romance in sight.

Sexual attraction was like that, he got it, but, seeing Jade twisting a strand of hair around her finger and transferring her weight from side to side, he suddenly felt like a heel.

He'd said she deserved better at Glacier Point this morning. The way he'd been behaving, that definitely applied to him too.

He'd initially planned on taking her out for dinner as a way to make up for how he'd been treating her the last month, a small gesture to show her he wasn't a complete bastard.

But here, now, seeing her dressed up, her expression guarded yet expectant, he knew he was deluding himself.

He'd said she deserved better earlier today and she did. Much better than what she'd put up with from him.

Dinner wouldn't just be a trite apology. Dinner would be the kind of date she deserved.

'You hungry?'

Nodding, she patted her tummy. 'Surprised you didn't mistake the rumbles for a stray grizzly.'

'Ah, so that's what that dull roar is.'

She laughed, the pure, joyful sound making him want to sweep her into his arms, twirl her around, and laugh out loud for the sheer pleasure of it.

Hitching her handbag higher on her shoulder, she said, 'Come on, then, feed me.'

In that split second, he was instantly transported back to the night he'd done exactly that; hand-feeding her that strawberry… and what followed…

Their gazes locked, her eyes wide, luminous, knowing, the faint blush staining her cheeks telling him she was remembering too.

He had no doubt if he headed down memory lane with her right now they'd end up where he wanted to be: in bed, having mind-blowing sex all night.

So much for romancing the lady.

He wanted to take her on a first date she'd remember. Looked as if his gallantry had fled around the time his libido had shot into the stratosphere.

Clearing his throat, he wrenched his gaze away with effort, feigned nonchalance as he glanced at his watch.

'We've got reservations, let's go.'

She nodded, but not before her lips curved in a tempting smile that said she knew exactly what he'd been thinking and maybe she wasn't averse to joining in the fun.

'Rhys?'

'Yeah?'

'Thanks for this.'

He squirmed under her admiration. 'For what? Letting you crash here rather than a hotel?'

'For Glacier Point. For being human. For letting me in again.'

Swivelling on her heel, she headed for the door, but not before he'd seen the depth of emotion shimmering in her eyes.

Damn straight he'd let her in again. At what cost? Could he slam the door on his past, with her help?

Filled with familiar doubt, he followed her.

As Jade slid into the chair Rhys held out for her and glanced around the restaurant he'd chosen she couldn't help but wonder what he'd do next to surprise her.

When he'd said he'd made reservations she'd expected a fancy upmarket place like the bar they'd visited their first night in Skagway, something fitting with his palatial home and upscale condo carved into a mountain.

Instead, he'd brought her to what could only be the smallest, oldest restaurant in town, a quaint wood-panelled lounge-like place with an open fireplace, mounted moose heads and stuffed salmon over the mantle and a collection of mismatched, dusty wine bottles along the back shelf of a makeshift bar.

There couldn't have been more than eight tables crammed into the place, yet the artfully arranged dividers provided some privacy for diners. Rather than fancy polished silverware and snowy-white crockery, the tables were covered in faded gingham and massive clay-based serving dishes that resembled platters rather than plates.

As he slid her chair in he leaned down, murmured in her ear, 'Don't let appearances fool you. This is the best restaurant in Skagway.'

She'd already been fooled by appearances once; no way

would she base the rest of her life on prejudging anything or anyone again.

As he sat opposite she folded her hands on the table, leaned forward. 'I like it. It's cosy.'

'Home away from home.'

Regret fluttered in her chest for a moment before she ignored it. While her parents had hurt her with their attitude, she still missed them. They'd been close, her sharing in their dazzling society life from the time she could walk and, while she preferred the simple, unadorned beauty of Alaska, she couldn't help but wish she'd arrived here under different circumstances.

A tiny crease appeared between his brows. 'I've said the wrong thing, dredged up bad memories.'

'No, it's okay.' She shook her head, smiled. 'Nothing like a home-cooked meal.'

His answering smile sent her heart into a free fall she had no hope of recovering from. 'If your mum's anything like mine, when did you last have a home-cooked meal?'

'When the caterers whipped up an old-fashioned, hearty Osso Bucco, of course.'

They laughed, the cosiness of the restaurant, their relaxed conversation, the intimacy of having dinner with him like a real date, suddenly overwhelming.

Some of what she was feeling must've shown on her face for he reached out, cupped her cheek briefly before signalling to a waiter.

'You happy for me to order?'

'Sure.'

Right now, she could be served polar bear and she wouldn't notice what she was eating. Cool, reserved, stand-offish, business-focused Rhys was tempting enough. Laid-back, warm, relaxed Rhys made her want to grab his hand, make a break from the restaurant and run all the way back to his condo.

In the space of a few hours, it was as if the last month hadn't happened. Her initial fury at how he'd pushed her away after their sensational night together, his driving her like a maniacal boss, his brusque treatment, had all faded under his understanding at Glacier Point and now, here, the tension between them was a thing of the past; replaced by a tension of another sort.

She knew what would happen tonight. In letting him into her heart again, she'd let him into her bed too. Nothing surer. And by the way he kept looking at her, with barely concealed hunger, he wanted to be there.

'Dinner shouldn't be too long.'

'Good.'

He raised an eyebrow, waiting for her to elaborate as she wished she could be more brazen and tell him the exact reason behind her wish for a speedy dinner.

Instead, she patted her tummy. 'I'm starving.'

The laugh lines at the corners of his eyes crinkled. 'In that case, you'll do justice to the rib eye.'

'And what's for dessert?'

She flung it out there as a dare, wondering if he'd allude to the last time they'd shared dessert and what had happened afterwards.

Not disappointing, his hand snaked across the table, traced a slow, sensual line along the back of hers, ending at her pulse, leaping all over the place.

'Depends what you fancy.' His blue eyes locked on hers, he murmured, 'I'm sure I could rustle up some strawberries and chocolate back at the condo.'

Heat streaked up her arm, zapped her, jump-starting every cell in her body craving his touch.

'My favourite,' she managed to say in response, her skin tingling with yearning.

'I remember.'

His slow, sexy smile lit her up from within and it took every ounce of willpower not to suggest they skip the main and head home for a healthy serving of dessert.

The arrival of their grilled rib eyes saved her from making any embarrassingly indecent proposals and she concentrated on cutting and forking the perfectly cooked beef into her mouth, trying not to squirm under his openly assessing gaze the entire time.

After scoffing half her steak, she forced herself to slow down. Building anticipation and all that.

'This is nice.'

'The meal or me not biting your head off for a change?'

Surprised he'd broached how he'd treated her the last month, she laid down her cutlery.

'You made your point clear after the night we…' She cleared her throat, subduing a grin at his guilty expression. 'The last month was all about business. I get that.'

'But I've been a real pain in the butt about it and you've done nothing but suck it up and work harder.'

He stabbed a piece of steak with extra force. 'I admire you for that.'

Folding her arms, she put on her best smug expression. 'Careful there, Ranger, almost sounded like a compliment.'

'You deserve it.'

She only just caught his muttered, 'And more.'

Buoyed by his honesty—not many guys would admit they were anything other than perfect—she decided to push her luck.

'Know what else I deserve?'

'A raise?'

She smiled. 'That too. Actually, I was thinking more along the lines of a stress-free weekend, totally work free.'

His eyebrows shot up. 'That's a bit hard, considering we're here to replenish stocks.'

Sending him a coy glance from beneath her lashes, she said, 'I'm willing to compromise. How about we balance work and play?'

'Play, huh?'

'Yep.'

She nodded her head emphatically, wondering if he'd join in the fun or revert to his bossy best.

When she glimpsed the corners of his mouth twitch, she knew she'd won.

Leaning forward, he crooked his finger. 'So tell me, what does this play involve?'

Stifling a laugh, she waved a hand in an airy gesture. 'I'm sure you've got loads of stuff at your condo.'

'Indoor play, huh?'

Jerking her head towards the frosted restaurant front, she nodded. 'As much as I love nature, I've spent the last few months outdoors. Time for a little fun inside.'

'What if I don't have any board games?'

This time, she crooked a finger at him, held up her hand and spoke behind it in an exaggerated conspiratorial whisper. 'I'm sure we can come up with some other form of entertainment.'

His eyes darkened with pleasure. 'I'm sure we can. But after the way I've treated you, I'd understand completely if you wanted to pick up your bat and ball and go home.'

With a confident toss of her head, she said, 'Where's the fun in that?'

His gaze dropped to her lips, lingered until they tingled, before sweeping back to meet her eyes.

'In that case, let's finish our dinner and let the games begin.'

She didn't have to be asked twice. The succulent beef, garlic-infused eggplants and roasted red onions with tarragon and olives were sublime, but the moment she'd eaten the last tasty morsel she was ready to grab the bill and leave.

Matching her urgency, he stood, came around to her side of the table and squeezed her shoulder. 'I'll take care of the bill, meet you at the front.'

Standing, she ended up toe to toe with him, his radiant heat palpable and almost making her swoon. Any excuse to place her hands on his rock-hard chest to steady herself.

'Thanks for dinner.'

'My pleasure.'

Laying a palm flat against his chest, she murmured, 'Soon to be all mine.'

He all but ran for the bill.

Jade hummed a Destiny's Child song about being an independent woman as she waited for Rhys to grab their coats.

An apt song, considering that was exactly how she felt right this very minute. She'd survived her first stretch in the wilds of Alaska, in her first job, with a boss who'd driven her hard.

Her hands were wrecked, her feet had blisters on their blisters and her back would never be the same again, yet she'd loved every minute of it. Every twinge, every ache, every niggle, was a testament to her trying her hardest and doing things her way. And having Rhys notice, let alone acknowledge her efforts, filled her with pride.

His honest appraisal of her efforts along with his unfettered admiration had been more of an aphrodisiac than his lowered barriers, allowing his natural charm to shine through.

She still had it bad for her boss.

Tonight, she'd show him just how much.

'Here you go.'

He held her coat open and she slid her arms into it, her heels slipping on the wet floorboards of the restaurant's entrance as she flailed for a second before he righted her, so strong, so dependable, so deliciously male.

'What's that you were humming?'

'Didn't you recognise my Beyonce imitation?'

His lips twitched. 'Uh, no.'

Emboldened by the two brandies she'd consumed with dinner, she batted her eyelashes. 'Too bad. Maybe I was humming something sexy?'

His blue eyes twinkled. 'Personally, I'd rather be doing than humming.'

The last time they'd slept together it had ended in disaster, their frigid working relationship rivalling the local glaciers in the frosty stakes. Now, she was under no illusions. They were away from their work place, their ever-present attraction was simmering and they were staying together in a luxurious condo. She didn't need a calculator to do the math.

The nervous flutter in her gut intensified as she laid a hand against his chest, feeling his pounding heart matching hers as she stood on tiptoe, her lips hovering an inch from his.

'Then what are we waiting for?'

With a faux growl he picked her up and hoisted her over his shoulder as if she weighed less than a sack of kindling.

'Are you nuts? Put me down!'

Laughing, she pummelled his back, ducking her head as a few couples on the opposite sidewalk applauded.

'Faster this way, what with you wearing stilts.'

He had a point. Besides, a small part of her liked his caveman act. His spontaneity turned her on, big time.

He stiffened as she slid her hands down his back and came to rest on his bottom.

'What are you doing?'

'Checking my mode of transport.' She patted his butt for good measure. 'Hope it's reliable enough to get me home.'

His grip on the back of her thighs tightened. 'Sweetheart, if you keep your hands there, this engine is guaranteed to run all night.'

Enjoying their banter despite practically hanging upside down, she groped his glutes, chuckling at his muttered oath. 'Mmm… reliability, style, class. Lucky me.'

'You forgot to mention great at handling curves.'

His hands skated up an inch, caressing her thighs, leaving a scorching imprint.

'What about in the wet?'

He stopped dead, slid her down his body, nice and slow, every inch of her screaming for him to repeat it with the two of them naked.

He tipped her chin up, his lips grazed hers, heartbreakingly gentle, softly seductive before he eased away, looked her straight in the eyes.

'You'll have to take me for a test-drive to find out.'

They stood on the doorstep to his condo, heat crackling between them. Jade knew the moment she stepped through the door, there'd be no turning back.

'I was never any good at gear changes. Might need a little help?'

She melted beneath the intensity of his stare, her body on fire, her resolve to not head down this track again shredded around the time she'd confided in him earlier today.

Somewhere between rocking the boat their first time in that damn canoe and trusting him enough to discuss her warped family, she'd fallen for him.

Every gorgeous, rebellious, infuriating inch of him.

Sliding an arm around her waist, he pulled her close, leaving her in no doubt how willing he was to help her take their driving analogy to the next level.

'Let's see if practice makes perfect.'

CHAPTER FIFTEEN

As RHYS backed Jade into the condo, slamming the door shut with his foot, reality hit.

She was about to sleep with the guy she'd fallen in love with.

Labelling it sex would've been much easier, much safer. Now, she'd be invested every step of the way.

Sensing her jitters, he ran his hands up and down her arms, warming, comforting. 'Fancy a hot tub before bed?'

He was trying to romance her all the way and she loved it, but the thought of sharing a hot tub with a guy who epitomised sex on legs was doing crazy things to her insides. Butterflies wouldn't even come close to what she was feeling. Try a dozen hamsters running on a wheel. No, try a dozen hamsters doing cartwheels, star-jumps and somersaults.

Silently telling the hamsters to take a flying leap, she nodded. 'Sure, sounds good.'

He brushed his thumb across her bottom lip, making it quiver. 'See you out there.'

The moment he released her and headed into the master bedroom she sank onto a chair, afraid her legs wouldn't support her. Pressing her fingers to her eyes, she took several deep breaths.

Hot guy. Hot tub. Hot stuff.

Belatedly, she added, *Hotfooting it out of here when he realises I'm in love with him.*

'You're not ready yet?'

She glanced up, her breath catching in her throat. Clothed,

Rhys was pretty darn hot. Semi-naked, he was simply magnificent: lean, well muscled, tanned all over.

Grasping at any excuse, she patted her tummy, mentally cringing when she realised she'd done the same thing a few hours earlier.

'I stuffed myself at dinner, just giving it a chance to settle.'

By his dubious expression, he didn't buy it for a second.

'Don't be too long. My engine's idling—I could definitely do with some revving up.'

Chalking one in the air for scoring another car analogy point, he strutted out to the hot tub, looking a million bucks and knowing it.

Cheeky devil.

Quashing her doubts, she headed for the bedroom, belatedly realising she had a problem. No swimsuit.

'Damn,' she muttered, rifling through her overnight bag in the vain hope that one might miraculously appear, her hand landing on a bra...*bingo*!

Six months in the Alaskan wilderness called for sensible underwear so she'd traded her lust for La Perla and settled for old-fashioned cotton. Thankfully, she'd relented and packed two eye-catching satin numbers, one black, the other red. After all, a girl never knew when she needed to reaffirm her femininity.

Stripping quickly, she donned the black ensemble and glanced in the mirror. Yowza! Her breasts spilled over the top of the bra cups and the scanty briefs barely covered what they were supposed to. Then again, what choice did she have? Barely black or skinny dipping?

'It's all in the attitude,' she muttered, strutting towards the balcony.

However, once she reached the sliding door she faltered. While the twinkling lights of Skagway glittered like gems scattered across a midnight, velvet carpet, the sight of Rhys reclining in the hot tub, head tilted back, eyes half-closed, easily rivalled the view.

With a deep breath she stepped out onto the balcony, his eyes snapping open at her footfall. He sat up slowly, his gaze travelling from head to foot, lingering everywhere in between.

'Come on in. The water's great.'

She didn't need a second invitation. The way he stared at her, she wanted to submerge and hide beneath the water before she stripped off and gave him a real show.

'Ooh…nice.' Sinking into the water, she settled on the bench seat within touching distance.

They'd been building towards this all night, no point going all coy now despite her serious attack of the jitters.

He picked up a bottle from a nearby ice bucket, poured a glass of champagne and handed her the delicate crystal flute.

'That's some outfit you're almost wearing.'

Inwardly wincing when her hand trembled, she raised the flute in his direction. 'Didn't think I'd be swimming in Alaska so this will have to do.'

'Oh, it does, very nicely,' he said, his exaggerated wink making her laugh.

She sipped at the champagne, savouring the icy bubbles sliding down her parched throat, her gaze fixed on Rhys over the rim of her glass, her pulse roaring.

After the brandy she'd had earlier a champagne chaser probably wasn't a great idea, but tell that to her heart, her gullible, impressionable, breakable heart that was lapping up every moment of tonight.

'I have a proposition for you.'

She drained the rest of her champagne in two gulps.

He'd turned up the bubbles, the powerful jets enhancing the tingling sensations racing across her sensitised skin, which had little to do with the water and everything to do with the gleam in his eyes.

Pretending she was propositioned in hot tubs by hot guys every day of the week, she sat back, draped her arms across the top of the tub.

'I bet you have.'

He chuckled. 'I wanted to make tonight special, kind of like the first date we never had. And you mentioned making this weekend a mixture of business and pleasure earlier. So how about we forget about the restocking awaiting us tomorrow and concentrate on the rest of the night, no doubts, no second-guessing, just the two of us enjoying our time together? Deal?'

She didn't hesitate when he held out his hand and as it closed over hers, his thumb circling her palm, it was as if she'd just made a deal with the devil himself.

Tugging on her hand, he said, 'I think it's time you sat over here. I won't bite…unless you want me to.'

His intoxicating grin held a hint of things to come as he pulled her across the tub and onto his lap.

'Much better,' he murmured as he leaned towards her.

His lips brushed hers, agonisingly slow. Her thighs trembled as his hands spanned her waist and pulled her closer, if that were possible.

'You're so beautiful,' he whispered against the side of her mouth, as he covered her face with feather-light kisses.

Burying her hands in his hair, she tugged him closer, wriggled in his lap, wrapping her legs tightly around him, pressing against his arousal. Her hips convulsed as he ground against her and she whimpered as he slid his tongue in her mouth, teasing her with infinite slowness. He licked and explored, daring her tongue to join his.

The kiss deepened and she was lost. She could no more stop this avalanche of all-consuming passion than walk on steady legs at this point in time.

'I want you, now.' She tore her mouth away, nuzzled his neck, nipping him, daring him with her teeth.

'I'm all yours.'

His roughened voice sent chills down her spine as he lay back, his lust-filled gaze riveted to her chest. Her breasts tingled as he reached out and gently traced the outline of each nipple with his index finger, the hardened buds straining against satin. She gasped, slivers of heat shooting from her nipples to her slick centre. She arched towards him, craving more. So much more.

Sensing her need, he slipped the straps off her shoulders. She was fired by the adoration in his eyes; her hands moved of their own volition. She wanted to be naked in front of him, to feel his hands against her flesh. She unhooked the bra and watched it float away on a cloud of bubbles. He moaned, long and low. He cupped one breast and licked around the nipple, round and round. Agonisingly slow. His tongue teased her into a frenzy.

As he lavished attention on her breasts, kneading, stroking, licking, sucking, she grew dizzy from the pure pleasure. The pulsating water jets, combined with his erotic assault, had her on the edge. And she didn't want to fall. Not yet. When she did, she wanted him with her all the way.

Her hand snaked under the water and he stiffened as she found her intended target. His hard thickness aroused her further as she slid her hand into his briefs. She grasped the shaft and started stroking with infinite tenderness.

'We have to get indoors before I lose it,' he muttered.

In response, she intensified her pressure, glorying in her powers to stimulate him.

Rhys watched Jade's tongue flick out and lick her top lip. Right then, with her hand stroking him and her bare breasts merely inches from his face, he almost exploded.

'Hey, slow down, I left my raincoat inside.'

Realisation dawned in her brown eyes, which had darkened to the colour of rich, dark chocolate.

'I didn't think about protection.' Her hand stilled. 'Your fault. I can't think straight at the moment.'

He traced her lips with a fingertip, his breath catching when she nibbled the end of his index finger before swirling her tongue around the tip, drawing it into her lush mouth, sucking it until he almost came.

'Let's go.'

He swung her up in his arms, revelling in the feel of her slender frame. She snuggled into him, nuzzling his neck. He was rock hard. And he was about to lose control.

She clung to him, her arms wound tightly around his neck.

'My hero,' she sighed, tracing a slow line down his cheek to his jaw with her fingertip.

He cradled her glistening body, soft and warm and pliant in

his arms, and his jaw clenched against a surge of emotion that left him weak and vulnerable, two emotions he'd vowed to never acknowledge again. But as she gazed at him with shimmering brown eyes, so adoring, so trusting, he felt ten feet tall.

Tonight would be all about her.

Placing her carefully on the king-size bed, he disengaged her arms, only to pin them to her sides. Her lips quirked in a wicked smile a second before he kissed her, invading her mouth swiftly and surely, taking and giving. Tearing his mouth away, he trailed a line of hot, moist kisses between her breasts to her navel.

'Rhys, please,' she begged softly, her breathing ragged as she squirmed, and he finally released her arms, her hands instantly grabbing hold of his shoulders and pulling his head down for more long, decadent kisses.

'Patience, sweetheart,' he whispered against her mouth before heading south, nibbling his way down her body, deliberately avoiding her sensitive breasts to heighten her desire, lingering on her navel, laving the indentation with his tongue as his fingertips skimmed the soft skin on the inside of her thighs.

She writhed beneath him, arching her pelvis towards his hungry mouth. He didn't need to be asked twice, moving down, inhaling the sweet, musky scent of her arousal. Hooking his thumbs into the elastic waistband of her black satin knickers, he ripped them off in one smooth movement, heard her draw in a sharp breath as he gazed at nirvana.

She whimpered as he pleasured her with his tongue, probing, delving, circling until she fisted her hands in his hair and screamed his name.

'Jeez…' She blew out a long, low whistle, her face flushed as she stared at him in wonder. 'That was freaking unbelievable.'

'And it was only the beginning.'

Standing, he gazed in awe at the goddess lying sprawled on the bed, droplets of water clinging to every delicious curve and dripping onto the cream coverlet. Her tousled hair laid spread above her, a crowning halo, as her rosy, swollen, thoroughly kissed lips beckoned.

She smiled at him then, a slow, seductive smile that set his heart hammering and his hand reaching across to the dresser and grabbing the foil pack.

'Let me do it.'

'You'll get no protests here.'

He gritted his teeth as she unrolled the condom over his rigid penis, her hands grazing his hard flesh in exquisite torture.

She lingered, taking her time, and he swore his eyes rolled back in his head when she neared the base.

He groaned and her gaze rose from his hard-on to meet his eyes and her wondrous expression stole his breath.

'I have plans for you.'

'What plans?'

Her eyes sparkled with mischief as she wrapped her hand around him and squeezed hard enough to make him jerk.

'A night you'll never forget.'

In an instant he covered her body with his, skin to delicious skin, his hardness fitting her softness. Taking a deep breath, he eased forward, nudging at her slick entrance, which promised to take him to heaven and back. He cupped her bottom with both hands and entered her in one smooth stroke. She gasped as he groaned at the sheer ecstasy of being inside her again. He moved slowly in and out, withdrawing and sinking deep again, his control on a knife edge.

She wrapped her legs around him, her soft panting moans urging him deeper, harder, faster, as he plunged into her again and again until he was spent, watching her breasts quiver with the impact of each thrust, his excitement mounting to excruciating levels.

'Rhys…oh, yeah…'

They bucked wildly, spasms ripping through his body at the same time she tightened and convulsed around him. The world exploded and for the first time in his life he saw stars. It was the orgasm to end all orgasms and he owed it all to the woman lying beneath him.

Sex with her a month ago had been mind-blowing but what had just happened defied logic.

Then again, since she'd strutted into his life the way he'd behaved, how he felt, had been far from logical.

And deep down, in a place locked away for ever, he knew why tonight had been different.

They hadn't had sex. They'd made love and mentally whispering the *L* word, let alone acknowledging it, sent a shudder of terror through him.

'You okay?' he asked softly, brushing a kiss against her lips.

She nodded, as dazed as him. 'Wow.'

He chuckled, savouring the feeling of still being wrapped in her tight warmth. 'Yeah, it was like that, wasn't it?'

He rolled to one side, cradling her within his arms as they lay in silence, wrapped in their own thoughts. He was starting to worry when she finally spoke.

'So, what do you do on a second date?'

CHAPTER SIXTEEN

RHYS's mobile rang while Jade was filling the bath. He planned on joining her, but a glance at caller ID had him reaching for the phone.

'Hey, bro, long time no hear. Starr and the kidlets keeping you busy?'

'You said it.'

'So what's up?'

Callum's weary sigh set his sibling antenna on edge. 'Nothing. Just called to touch base. It's been a while.'

'Yeah, I've been busy too.'

Working the tours for the first time in two years, getting a handle on his guilt, denying his feelings for Jade. Real tiring stuff.

'How's Jade working out?'

'Great.'

He kept any hint of emotion out of his voice and thankfully his brother was too tired to pick up on his forced cheery response.

'I'm glad. With her lack of experience I had my reservations, but then I met her and I knew she was worth taking a risk on.'

'Yeah, considering how great she's been, Fred did me a favour in asking me to hire her. She's a model employee.'

A nasty shiver scuttled across the back of his neck. Jade had been so antagonistic towards her parents, so gung-ho about doing this on her own, proving her independence, if she ever discovered the truth he knew she'd start doubting herself again.

'Did you know he offered me a monetary incentive to hire her?'

Callum whistled low. 'No way.'

'Yeah. I didn't take it, though. Being pushed into employing her was bad enough. Thankfully it's worked out.'

Rhys rubbed the back of his neck. The truth behind her employee contract put him in a difficult position. As Jade's—what? Friend? Lover? Something more?—he owed her the truth. At what cost? Ruining all she'd achieved?

He knew her. She'd ignore all the great work she'd done over the last few weeks and focus on the one small fact dear Daddy had pulled a few strings to get her the job in the first place.

'Then what's the problem?'

Apart from the fact he'd fallen for her, had to tell her the truth and risk undoing all the ground he'd made up over the last twenty-four hours?

'No problem.'

Callum cleared his throat, a clear sign he was hedging around something. 'Starr wants to know when you're going to meet the twins.'

He stiffened, clutched the phone to his ear before deliberately rolling his shoulders out. 'Soon.'

'That's what you've said since their birth.'

He heard the disappointment in his brother's tone and, for a second, wished things were different. But he'd been this way for too long, had survived because of it, and changing habits of a lifetime was damn tough; not to mention downright scary.

He knew what would happen if he met the twins. He'd fall for their funny forthrightness, their exuberant boisterousness, the inbuilt ability all kids had to love and trust. He'd been like that once, hated how scarred and cynical he'd become.

Growing attached to the twins wouldn't be a good idea and would only serve to strengthen the emotional ties to his brother, something he would've given anything for once but which now scared him beyond belief. The pain of losing Archie had devastated him; losing Callum too would be incomprehensible.

As he searched for the right words to ease the tension between them an image of Jade, lying in his arms last night, popped into his head.

He wanted more nights like the one they'd had last night. Many more. But she'd be leaving, heading back to Australia, and he didn't believe in relationships, never mind long-distance ones.

Yet the thought of losing her ripped a hole the size of Davidson Glacier in his heart. A heart he'd already opened to a sassy, determined, beautiful woman. Why not go the whole hog and let his family in too? Face his fears. Become the man he was before grief and the pain of loss had slammed his emotional barriers firmly in place. Maybe he could schedule a visit to meet his niece and nephew shortly after Jade returned to Oz?

'I'll be there in the next few months.'

'Uh-huh.'

He couldn't blame Callum for his doubt. He deserved it. What kind of an idiot was he to deliberately stay away from the only family he valued because he was too damn scared?

'I mean it this time, bro.'

Some of his conviction must've relayed to Callum for he could've sworn he heard his smile.

'Great, I'll tell Starr and the kids.'

That sealed it. His dedicated, responsible brother would never involve his kids unless he truly believed him.

'Say hi to them for me. I'll be in touch soon.'

'Great. Bye.'

Feeling as if he'd shrugged off a few years' worth of emotional baggage he'd been lugging around, he grinned, ready to join Jade in the bathroom.

As he turned his happiness evaporated. Jade stood in the doorway, wearing a towel and a frown. A big one.

'Tell me you weren't talking about me.'

Taking a step towards her, he held up his hands. 'Listen—'

'No!'

She paled, clutched at the doorframe, and he reached her side in two seconds flat.

'I was going to tell you—'

'No, no, no…' she mumbled, shaking her head, slumped against the wall.

'Jade, please, come sit down, let me explain—'

'Don't touch me!'

She shoved him away when he tried to bundle her into his arms, her posture rigid, resistant, as he silently cursed for not telling her the truth sooner.

Helpless, he balled his hands into fists, thrust them into his pockets, waited until she looked at him, the depth of her pain slicing into whatever lingering doubts he might have had about his feelings for her.

He wouldn't feel this lousy if he didn't love her, and the realisation threatened to send him running from the condo without looking back. He had form. That was what he'd always done.

But the glimmer of tears in her devastated eyes, the agonising twist to those lips he adored, guaranteed he'd ignore his first instinct and do something completely out of character this time.

He'd stay.

'Listen to me. You've done a brilliant job, everything you've achieved has been you, one hundred per cent you. Not your interfering dad, *you*.'

Her bottom lip trembled and his precarious hold on not blurting out his feelings for her here and now seriously wobbled.

'Don't you get it? I never would've got the job if he hadn't called in a favour. And *you* went along with it!'

Tears spilled down Jade's cheeks, agony slicing her heart in two.

Everything she'd done over the last weeks, everything she'd achieved, meant nothing, pride in her new-found independence crumbling under the weight of discovery.

She hadn't got the job on her own.

None of this was real.

Every blister, every splinter, every back spasm, had been relished as evidence of how far she'd come from her old life. Ironic, as this new life she'd striven for and made for herself was as much a sham as the old one.

The icing? The man she'd fallen for was in on it from the very beginning.

Swallowing the great wrenching sobs that threatened to spill out, she knuckled her eyes, wishing this were all a nightmare and when she woke up she'd be back in Rhys's arms, secure in his bed, happier than she'd ever been.

Sadly, when she opened her eyes, the reality smacked her in the face all over again.

Rhys paced, stopping in front of her, reaching out to her, his hands falling uselessly to his sides when she deliberately stepped out of reach.

'You have to believe me.' Dragging a hand through his hair, he shook his head, his tortured expression surely matching hers. 'Callum said you impressed the hell out of him at the screening interview. And don't forget you did the same to me. I'm the CEO, I had the final say.'

'Bull. You only hired me because you had to.' She jabbed a finger in his direction, fury making her hand tremble. 'What was it you said on the phone? He offered you money! Jeez—'

'I never contemplated taking it—'

'And what was this bloody *favour* he called in?'

Shaking her head, the tears sprayed like a sprinkler of misery. 'What did you owe him?'

Sadness clouded his eyes. 'Your dad helped send a few cruise-line referrals my way. In the business world, one good deed often leads to another, so when he called me up out of the blue, saying his only kid needed a job and it happened to coincide with a vacancy here, I took you on.'

'I knew it was a crock, all of it.'

Swinging around, she caught a glimpse of herself in the bath-room mirror: wet, lank hair framing her tear-blotched face, eyes red-rimmed from crying, mouth mutinous. She looked like a woman who'd lost everything she believed in, again.

He laid a hand on her shoulder and she shrugged it off, swing-ing back to face him, on the attack.

'I thought what I'd achieved was real and it's worthless! All of it!'

Unfazed, he held his hands out to her, palm up. 'Don't you get it? Regardless of your dad calling in a favour I never would've hired you if I didn't think you were capable.'

He lowered his voice, his earnestness reinforcing his words, words she wanted to believe but couldn't. 'And every single minute since, you've shone. You've risen to every challenge I set, you never gave up, you pushed harder and longer than any other employee I've ever had. With no experience!'

Going for broke, he pinned her with his most beseeching stare. 'Honestly? I was extra critical of you right from the very start. Firstly, because I was resentful of having to hire you on the whim of your dad. Secondly, because I expected you to be an uptight princess slumming it for a while.'

She squared her shoulders in outrage as he rushed on. 'But you blew every preconception sky-high, with your dogged determination, your guts and your sheer bloody-minded perseverance.'

A small fragment of her heart cracked as he tilted her chin to stare into her eyes.

'Quite simply, sweetheart, you're the best.'

While her body remained rigid, some of her anger melted clean away. She valued his honesty and how it made her feel: as if the last few months weren't a complete waste of time.

She *had* tried hard, had given her all, and to hear how much he appreciated it…well, it went some way to making up for his part in all this. Though he wasn't directly the bad guy he'd known about it, she'd trusted him, had thought he was different, so a small part of her felt doubly betrayed.

'I'm the best, huh? Really?'

'Really.'

Rhys kissed Jade, a soft, tender kiss designed to soothe and distract and comfort, a kiss to reinforce every true word he'd just spoken.

His admiration for what she'd achieved knew no bounds and even now, when faced with what she'd see as treachery, she'd given him a fair hearing, was willing to listen despite how devastated she must be feeling.

When the kiss ended their lips clung, lingered, reluctant to break the bond that hovered between them, unsaid, despite the test he'd unwittingly just put them through.

'Thanks for the pep talk.'

'No pep talk.' He smacked his chest. 'Came right from here.'

'But it doesn't change what I have to do.'

She crossed to the window, her rigid posture scaring him. Seeing the bath sheet wrapped around her body, skimming her thighs, showed him exactly how far gone he was. He'd just kissed a semi-naked woman and all he'd thought about was assuaging her injured feelings.

'Jade?'

She turned slowly, the resolute set to her chin, the determination in her eyes terrifying him.

'I have to quit.'

'What?'

He leaped as if a grizzly had bit his butt, stalked towards her, but stopped short of hauling her into his arms when she backed away.

'This job was always about experience. I have that now. It's time.'

Desperate, he clutched at straws. 'But your employment contract—'

'Was based on a flexible trial.' She shook her head. 'We both know where we stand.'

He didn't get this, any of it. Sure, he understood her motivation. He hadn't wanted a bar of Cartwright Corporation, hadn't wanted a single thing from dear old Dad; discounting his thirst for affection as a kid. So, yeah, he understood the desire for independence, the need to prove herself, but the thought of her leaving now, when he'd just discovered his true feelings…he couldn't let her go.

'You can't go.'

He grabbed her arms, held on tight, wishing he could never let go.

'You can't make me stay.'

Those five words didn't slay him half as much as the bleakness in her voice.

She was right, he couldn't. What right did he have?

Taking his silence as agreement, she shook off his hands. 'I'll finish the next fortnight of tours, but after that, I'm gone.'

A familiar ache clamped his heart, spread across his chest, numbing him, until he wondered if he was having a heart attack for real. But he dismissed the fleeting thought in an instant.

He knew this feeling, the same heartbreaking, gut-wrenching agony that had followed Archie's death, Claudia's death, the same helplessness that nothing he said or did could undo or change a thing.

He wanted to tell her everything. Hell, he wanted to beg her to stay. But he couldn't find the right words, let alone force air past the tightness in his throat.

So he stood there, the ache in his chest spreading, insidious and devastating, as she clutched the towel to her chest, stepped around him and padded across the floor.

He waited until he heard the bedroom door close before collapsing onto the couch, rubbing furiously at his aching chest.

It didn't help. Nothing would, not this time.

He was through running.

Ironic, the only time he'd ever stood still long enough he'd fallen in love. With a woman determined to do what he'd been doing for a lifetime.

Spread her wings.

Prove her independence.

And run without looking back.

CHAPTER SEVENTEEN

JADE hated goodbyes.

It wasn't enough she had to leave a dream job; she had to farewell the man she loved too.

She'd tried hating Rhys after discovering his treachery, had summoned up every ounce of latent anger at his betrayal.

She'd opened up to him about doubting her own judgement when everything went pear-shaped in her life so felt doubly betrayed now, her confidence seriously shaken. Was her judgement so off that the guy she'd thought was different was in fact another bad judgement call on her part?

She'd trusted him, he'd let her down, like every other person she'd loved in her life.

Then the initial anger had faded and she'd been more realistic. Rhys might have lied to her at the start, but when it counted he'd come clean, still supportive of her, whereas her folks and Julian had expected her to accept whatever they dished her way and put up with it.

So much of what he'd said had rung true. While she'd harboured a dream when she'd first arrived, a small part of her had expected it to be easy, like everything else that had fallen into her lap her whole life. She *had* been a pampered society princess, who was now ashamed of giving up her ideals, her dreams, in exchange for a cushy ride down easy street.

She couldn't blame him for thinking the same. But she could blame him for not telling her the truth, for letting her fall for him regardless.

She was through. Time to take her dream all the way: head back to Australia, enrol in university, gain her biology degree and start making a difference in the world, *her* way.

Besides, he didn't love her back. For as much as she wanted to prove her independence and follow her dream, she would've given it all up in a heartbeat if Rhys loved her back.

She'd given him the opportunity the day in his condo when she'd first discovered his treachery, when she'd told him she quit. He could've begged her to stay. She'd half hoped he would.

His response? Silence.

A silence he'd maintained over the last fortnight.

They'd worked together side by side every day, had shared a bed every night, lost in a desperate passion, making love like two people who knew they'd never see each other again.

But not many words had been spoken beyond the necessary; not the words that really mattered.

She hadn't cared. She'd taken what she could get, used their physical bond to soothe the constant ache of his betrayal deep inside. Not that she'd done herself any favours, for despite walking away every contour of his face, every nuance in his voice, every expression in his fathomless eyes, would stay imprinted on her soul for ever.

'You ready to go?'

Sucking in a deep breath and hoping her smile didn't wobble, she turned to face him.

'Yeah.'

'Sure you don't want me to head back to Skagway with you? We could—'

'Shh…' She placed her fingers against his lips, silencing him. 'Don't make this harder than it already is.'

Pain slashed his proud features before he quickly rearranged them in his usual confident mask. 'Okay.'

'I guess this is goodbye, then.'

She inwardly cringed. How trite, how inadequate, for what she really wanted to say.

A muscle twitched near his jaw. 'I guess so.'

Don't cry…don't cry…don't cry…

At the inevitable sting of tears she breathed deeply, willing them away while savouring the smell uniquely him. The scent of forest and outdoor and cool sunshine would always remind her of him, of this wild country that had captured her heart, as he had.

'Look after yourself. Call me if you need anything.'

'Thanks.'

She couldn't stand this, her nerves stretched to breaking point, a twang away from snapping.

'I better go.'

He nodded, his cool indifference surprising her after all they'd shared.

As she bent to pick up her backpack he reached out and their arms tangled in her hurry to fling herself into his.

She welcomed the frantic clash of mouths, her arms locking around his neck, her hands tangling in his hair, desperate to pull him closer, to never let him go.

He devoured her, exquisite, desperate, frantic kisses that made her knees buckle. She clung to him, unable to stand as he hugged her tight, squeezing out what little air was in her lungs.

'I won't ever forget you,' he murmured against her hair, hanging on for dear life before he broke the embrace, staring deep into her eyes for an infinite moment.

Time stood still, the crisp air around them crackling with the ever-present heat.

She wished he loved her.

She wished he'd ask her to stay.

Instead, he ducked down for one last, snatched kiss before turning and walking away.

Taking her heart with him.

Jade should've been happy.

Once she'd left Alaska she hadn't returned to Sydney, preferring to head to Melbourne—away from her family—and gaining acceptance into university there.

Thanks to her stint with Wild Thing and a glowing letter of recommendation from Rhys she'd scored a mature-student place in a biology degree course. Without any help from the blasted Beachams.

It should've been a proud moment, vindication she could achieve anything without their help and money. But all she could think about was how much more stimulating working in the field was compared to dry textbooks. Though she knew that had more to do with her personal park naturalist than the field itself.

Rhys haunted her. Every waking moment and most sleepless ones were filled with memories of him and as the days dragged by she faced reality.

He was no longer a part of her life.

A small, delusional part of her had secretly hoped he'd follow her back to Skagway, even to Vancouver before she left for Australia, professing his inability to live without her. No such luck. There'd been no contact whatsoever, not even a phone call.

She shouldn't be surprised. It was what he did: chalked it up to experience, moved on to the next one. He'd told her the truth from the start and she'd understood, but it didn't make the sorrow of losing him any easier. An anguish that persisted no matter how many hours she spent researching in the library or how many make-up tests she took.

While doing this course was her dream, she knew deep down part of her endless drive, her dedication to put in the long hours and survive on limited sleep, had more to do with obliterating the ever-present ache in her heart than a need to be top of her class.

Whatever she studied, she'd unwittingly relate it back to Rhys and what she'd learned in the field; a futile, masochistic habit that only served to dredge up her barely submerged devastation on a daily basis.

She hurt, constantly, an emotional pain that never went away no matter what she did.

She'd loved him. She'd lost him. She'd need to accept it, but for now the pain was too raw, too recent for her to do anything but bury herself in her studies and hope it would ease with time.

Then there was the parent issue. She hadn't told them she'd

returned to Australia and, surprisingly, Rhys couldn't have mentioned it to his brother, for if he had she had little doubt her dad would've heard the news and immediately hired a PI to find her.

For the first time in her life she was truly alone and, while she savoured the cushion of her trust fund set up by her granny years ago, enabling her to rent a semi-decent one-bedroom apartment not far from uni, she missed her family.

She'd spent a lifetime idolising them, loving them, being their darling and she missed them despite her shattered trust.

All the hours alone had given her loads of thinking time and, while she hadn't come to any definite conclusions, she'd mulled, a lot.

Had she overreacted? Not with Julian, for she'd never put up with any partner cheating on her, let alone a husband, but her parents?

They'd been married for many years, appeared happy, were the perfect couple. So she'd caught her dad having an affair? And her mum tolerated it? Who was she to judge?

What they did in their marriage was their business and now she'd had months away, had truly fallen in love for the first time, she knew what it was like to make sacrifices to keep a relationship running smoothly.

Hadn't she compromised during her last fortnight at Glacier Point? Throwing herself into whatever time they had left, ignoring the fact he'd lied to her right from the start and didn't love her enough to beg her to stay, taking what she could get?

She might not like the falsities of her parents' relationship, but it had nothing to do with her. She'd reacted like a spoilt little rich girl whose rose-coloured glasses got smashed, and it had taken time away and a broken heart to accept the fact she'd grown up.

Maybe it was for the best. If she hadn't had her eyes opened to reality she might've still been coasting along, believing the world was a perfect place, her folks the perfect role models and Julian the perfect fiancé.

She'd never believed in the old 'things happen for a reason' line, but in this case she'd had a lucky escape. While she didn't give a flying fig for Julian any more, she still loved her parents. Was it time to lay her judgemental prejudices aside and re-establish contact?

Screwing up her nose at the thought, she flipped open a botany textbook and picked up her pen to take notes.

She'd do it, after she aced this next test.

Rhys was at his wit's end. Ever since he'd returned from Alaska nothing had run smoothly.

While Aldo had been a competent CEO in his absence there was a multitude of problems that needed attending to. Cheri had handled the workload well, though she and Aldo seemed to spark off each other, something he hadn't noticed until now. And, to top it off, one of the major cruise lines was haggling over its contract.

Work wasn't the only problem. He hadn't slept in weeks. Sure, he caught a few z's here and there, but for the bulk of the nights an image of a stunning brunette with big brown eyes haunted him.

Letting her go at Glacier Point had been damn near impossible. It had ripped him apart. But he couldn't ask her to give up her dream, no matter how much he wanted to. Her father had already interfered in her quest for independence; he'd be damned if he did the same.

Acknowledging the truth and living with it were two entirely different things and, while he knew letting her go had been the right thing to do, it killed him, little by little, every day.

A loud knock had him throwing down his pen and stretching overhead.

'Come in,' he said, not in the mood for another problem.

The door cranked open and Cody popped his head around it. 'Hey, boss. How's it hanging?'

Smiling despite his foul mood, he gestured him in. 'Not too bad. You?'

Cody plonked into the chair facing him. 'Pretty good, though I'm missing Glacier Point something shocking.'

'Know what you mean. Didn't realise how much I'd missed it 'til I was back. Once it's in your blood, you're smitten for life.'

Cody leaned back and clasped his hands behind his head. 'Sure you're just talking about the scenery? Seems to me you were smitten with other…stuff.'

Swamped with memories of Jade, Rhys cleared his throat. 'She was something special, wasn't she?'

Jade's number-two fan—he had the number-one spot all sewn up—nodded. 'Yep, she was. Thought you two might've kept something going, what with her head over heels for you and all.'

Unsure whether Cody was speculating, he straightened. 'Head over heels?'

Cody chuckled. 'Like you didn't know? Hell, man, you were all she could talk about, not to mention how she looked whenever you were around. She lit up.'

He only just caught his, 'You lucky dog.'

'Did she say anything?'

'Not in so many words…'

'Spit it out!'

Cody held up his hands. 'Whoa! All she said was, as much as she wanted to be a biologist she would've given it up in a heartbeat to stay at Glacier Point, that's all. So I kinda assumed that meant with you?'

His heart pounded as he struggled to come to terms with what he'd just heard. 'She said that?'

Cody grinned. 'Yeah, cool, huh? You gonna do anything about it?'

He collapsed back, reeling from the truth.

Jade had been willing to give up her dream to stay in Alaska.

He hadn't wanted to say anything to her for fear of standing in the way of her dream.

But if she really felt like that…

A glimmer of an idea hovered at the edge of consciousness… She loved nature, she loved the cold. He needed to bring a smidgeon of all that to her life in Melbourne, needed to get her to remember the brilliant parts of being together in Alaska…

Something Callum had once told him resonated…hearing an avalanche survivor lecture in some weird ice cave…

The answer came to him in a flash of inspiration and he could've punched the air. It would be a cinch to organise: check the venue on the Internet, book it out, contact an online printer to send her a formal invitation she couldn't refuse… Oh, yeah, this would definitely work.

'By the look on your face, boss, you've hatched a plan.'

Buzzed for the first time in a long time, he smiled. 'Damn straight. About time I did something.'

Something he should've done weeks ago: tell Jade the truth and convince the woman he loved to take a chance on a guy like him.

Flipping the practice exam over, Jade sat back, sipped the dregs of her lukewarm coffee and grimaced. She'd been hard at it the last hour, had done as much studying as she could to pass this exam.

Time to move on to the next tough assignment of the night: ring her folks.

Rolling her shoulders, she shook out her hands and reached for her mobile. Now or never.

Punching the number, she waited, each prolonged ring exacerbating her nerves until she rubbed her tummy to settle the skating penguins doing figure-eights in there.

'Fred Beacham.'

The penguins skidded to a stop and crashed into a snow-bank, leaving her winded. Hearing her dad's voice after all this time did that to her and she bit her lip, hard, to stop it from wobbling.

'Hello?'

Sucking in a deep breath, she clutched the phone tighter. 'Dad, it's me.'

Silence. An awkward, heavy, drawn-out silence that frayed her already shredded nerves.

'I know it's been a long time—'

'Six months, give or take.' Her heart sank at his abrupt tone. 'How are you?'

'I'm fine. Back in Australia, thought it's time I called.'

'Where are you?'

'Melbourne. Enrolled in a biology course.'

'What happened to the job in Alaska?'

'Once I discovered you were behind me being employed, I quit.'

'I was only trying to help.'

'Funny, I saw it as interfering in my life when you knew going it alone was important to me.'

Her dad coughed, cleared his throat as she threw down her pen when she realised she was doodling love hearts with Rhys's initials on the back of her practice exam.

'I was worried. After what happened…I didn't know how to make amends…I wanted to make up for—'

'Dad, it's okay. I get it.'

'You do?'

'I was pretty angry at the time but I've had time to think—' boy, had she had time to think '—and I know you were trying to protect me.'

As her parents had always done. She'd led a charmed life, had been given everything she ever wanted, including her parents' unswerving devotion. When she'd confronted them, ranted at them, she could imagine how devastated they must've been. They'd presumably lost the one honest thing between them: her.

'I'm sorry I put you through all that business, honey. And your mother is too.'

'Apology accepted. Though you know I don't agree with any of it, right? Your affair, Mum's tolerance, her expecting me to be like her?'

Her dad cursed. 'I've been an old fool and I'd hate for you to think what your mother did is right. She should've booted me out a long time ago, should never have put up with my crap. I did wrong by her and there's no excuse for it.'

She didn't want to rehash her parents' private life, didn't want to dwell on how close she'd come to being trapped in a marriage that could've easily turned out the same.

Had she really been that blind? Or had she deliberately dwelled in the rosy world they'd created, content to ignore anything unsavoury, even a hint of it, so as not to rock the boat?

She'd mulled over this a lot the last few weeks while contemplating ringing her folks, had come to the unwelcome realisation that maybe she was to blame a little. She'd allowed her parents to shield her so she coasted along, content in her perfect life, in the lap of luxury, not actively pursuing her dream, then was outraged to learn her dad had a hand in getting her a job?

'That's your business, Dad. Guess I just wanted to touch base, let you know I'm back and maybe we can catch up once my exams are finished?'

'We'd love that, honey. You name the time and place, we'll be there.'

His voice caught and the last of her lingering resentment faded.

She'd never seen her dad cry. Big, bold, brash Beacham, Australia's top tycoon, never showed vulnerability, so to hear emotion in his voice showed her exactly how sorry he was.

'Great. I'll be in touch.'

'Jade?'

'Yeah?'

'We love you, honey.'

'Same here. Bye.'

Flinging the phone on the table, she linked hands and stretched overhead.

She'd done it, shifted the sadness weighing her down, taken the first step in re-establishing a relationship with her folks.

She should feel great. Instead, a spur of sorrow still lodged in her heart, niggling, annoying, hurting.

Sadly, she couldn't do anything about it. What she felt for Rhys Cartwright could not be solved with a phone call.

Her hand hovered over the phone lying face down on the table. It was a day for fresh starts; it was so tempting to call him.

And say what?

Hey, it's me, the idiot who fell so hard for you I'm still pining? The crazy woman who'd give up everything if you wanted me with you?

Yeah, bet that would go down a treat.

Shaking her head, she picked up the mobile and shoved it into her bag, right to the bottom, under a stack of texts and Post-It notes and fluorescent highlighters.

She'd extended enough olive branches for one day.

CHAPTER EIGHTEEN

DÉJÀ VU washed over Jade as she shrugged into a ski jacket, wiggled her fingers into gloves and slid her feet into Ugg boots.

She'd followed the same routine countless times in Alaska but hadn't expected to be doing the same in Melbourne in the middle of summer.

'Welcome to the Arctic Lounge, Miss Beacham. Head on through.'

She smiled at the doorman who'd checked her personal invitation and entered the funky ice bar in the middle of the CBD.

Having a chance to hear Sir Roland Hyde, the explorer who'd lived in Antarctica for the last decade and who'd just conquered Everest, was worth the hassle of getting rugged up.

Besides, as she glanced around the ice bar, she couldn't help but admire what some artistic person had done with thirty tonnes of ice. Everything was made from the stuff, from the bar to the couches to the glasses. Surreal.

'I believe you're expected in The Freezer Room, Miss Beacham. If you'll follow me?'

Impressed by the service, she followed the hostess—doing a mean Eskimo impersonation in her snazzy gear—through the bar to a room at the back.

She smiled her thanks as she entered, momentarily blinded by the strategically placed lighting reflecting off the ice.

Blinking, she refocused, only to see a mirage.

Okay, so she was seriously mixing up her desert and ice metaphors, but the man standing in the centre of the empty room wasn't Sir Roland.

He was an adventurer and had conquered more than mountains—namely her heart—and seeing him here, now, when she least expected it rooted her feet to the spot.

'It's great to see you.'

Five little words. That was all it took: her knees wobbled, her stomach somersaulted and the last few months apart faded into oblivion.

Her greedy gaze gobbled up every familiar contour of Rhys's face: those sharp cheekbones, angular jaw, blazing blue eyes and his mouth...

She couldn't speak, couldn't form the words, so she dragged in a frosty breath, his signature aftershave drowning her senses.

Divine. Intoxicating. All Rhys.

'Thanks.'

'For what?'

'For missing me.'

'What gives you that idea?'

He leaned down, kissed her cheek, softly, reverently, all too briefly.

'I can see it in your eyes.'

Capturing her face between his strong hands, he gave her no option but to meet his gaze, her heart leaping like a caged salmon. 'Or is it just a reflection of how much I've missed you?'

She wanted to bury her face in his chest, to hold him and squeeze him and never let go.

But that time had passed and she'd be better off looking at this for what it was: a wanderer probably paying a flying visit to his brother and looking up an old flame along the way.

'Whatever you're thinking, stop.'

He released her and she would've staggered if he hadn't grabbed hold of her arm and led her to an ice couch, some brown faux fur draped across its 'cushions'.

'Comfy?'

She shot him an 'are you kidding?' look. 'As comfy as I can be sitting on a giant ice block.'

He smiled at her grouchy tone. 'Didn't hear you complaining in Alaska.'

Mustering her best withering glare and hoping it didn't come out a squint, she stared him down. 'I didn't complain about a lot of things in Alaska I should've.'

He winced. 'You're talking about my stupidity in letting you go?'

'And the rest.'

He laughed, the rich timbre of his chuckles warming her despite the chill. 'I've missed that bluntness.'

'Not enough, obviously,' she muttered, tucking her gloved hands under her armpits for extra warmth—in reality, to stop from reaching out and touching him to see if he was real.

Sheepish, he briefly touched her thigh, dropping his hand when she stiffened. 'I would've been here sooner but I had a lot of stuff to sort out.'

'Work?'

'And this.'

He tapped his temple. 'I've been doing a lot of thinking.'

She didn't say a word, waited to see what he'd say.

When he muttered a curse, leaped to his feet and started pacing, she wasn't surprised. Discussing anything resembling emotion would be impossible to him. She should know.

'This is hard.'

She raised an eyebrow. 'What, talking to me?'

'Finding the right words despite rehearsing this a million times in my head.'

Cutting him some slack, she gestured around the room. 'You wouldn't have gone to all this trouble to get me here, what with the invitation and the fake lecture and all, if it wasn't important. So spill.'

Stopping dead, he jammed his hands in his pockets and shot her a wild-eyed look.

'I'm in love with you,' he blurted, his expression that of a deer cornered in a bear cave.

Her heart leaped before she beat it down with a good whack of common sense. She'd yearned to hear those words a few months ago but, in reality, what had changed?

She had a degree to complete, fences to mend with her family, a life to reassemble.

So, as much as she wanted to leap off the uncomfortable sofa and do cartwheels, his impassioned declaration changed nothing.

Jamming a hand through his hair, forgetting he had gloves on, elicited another curse. 'Say something.'

'Thanks.'

His jaw dropped. '*Thanks*? I fly halfway around the world, orchestrate this romantic meeting and you *thank* me?'

He searched her face for some sign, some clue that what he'd said had struck a chord. But she'd become a master at hiding her emotions this last year and was confident he'd find nothing.

'I'm wasting my time, aren't I?'

That was when she saw it, the flicker of raw, soul-slicing pain, the kind of pain she'd endured when she'd walked away from him at Glacier Point.

She couldn't speak, her throat clogged with regret and fear and pain. His face crumpled at her continued silence, his devastation a clear sign he cared as deeply as she did.

To his credit, he didn't move, didn't give up.

'Tell me to leave and I will.'

She should tell him to go. It would be the right thing to do, for there was no hope for them, not really. All that time spent together in Alaska hadn't been in vain. She'd listened to him, really listened, got to know him, and everything he'd said and done had clearly indicated he wasn't a guy to settle.

And that was what she wanted this time around.

To settle.

Her way.

Not for the sake of a fiancé's precious career, or the appearances of a wealthy family; she wanted a home and a family of her own and a guy who was crazy enough about her to never let her go.

She knew why he was here. He must've finished his stint in

Alaska, headed back to Vancouver and got a usual dose of itchy feet, so he'd hopped on a plane to Australia on the pretext of seeing her and his brother.

But why say he loves you?

Hmm…she hadn't quite figured out his motivation behind that yet.

Shaking his head, he dropped to one knee, grabbed her hand. 'Tell me.'

She opened her mouth to say the words to drive him away once and for all, to follow *her* dream for once.

But before she muttered a word, her bottom lip trembled and no amount of clamping it shut would stop.

Oh-oh. When her lip wobbled, the waterworks weren't far behind and she blinked. To no avail.

'Ah, hell,' Rhys muttered, rejoining her on the ridiculous ice sofa and bundling her into his arms. Where she belonged, where she ought to be for ever.

He'd botched this.

From the minute she'd caught sight of him and he'd seen her initial elation quickly masked by reservation, he'd bungled along, his famed control shot.

He'd rehearsed what he had to say, how to make her believe him, yet he'd made a hash of it and now she was crying.

Worse, she hadn't said she loved him. She'd thanked him, and even an emotional novice like him knew it didn't bode well when a woman you were crazy about thanked you for loving her.

He let her sob it out, smoothing her hair, rubbing her back through the ridiculously thick puffy parka.

Way to go with the romantic gesture. She was so bundled up he couldn't feel her body. And he desperately wanted to feel her. Not in a sexual way—though the memories of how they burned up the sheets was never far from his mind—but just to hold her, to feel her soft curves moulding to him.

Thankfully, her sobs soon petered out, and when they turned to the occasional hiccup he gently pulled back.

'You okay?'

She nodded, biting her bottom lip.

'You've hardly spoken two words. That's so not like you.'

Her lip wobbled into a smile. It was a start.

The way he saw it, she wouldn't be emotional if she didn't care. Tears were a good sign. Meant he still had a chance.

For the longer she'd let him hold her, the firmer his conviction grew.

He was through running.

If he didn't make a stand, right here, right now, he'd spend the rest of his life drifting.

One way or another, he'd get the answers he came for. And wouldn't budge an inch until he got them.

'Want to know why I arranged this here?'

She nodded, strands of her thick hair falling around her face, and he couldn't resist pushing them back behind her ear, cupping her cheek gently for a moment, silently cursing these damned gloves.

'Because I figured you'd need to get reacquainted with the cold again, seeing as I hoped you'd want to migrate to Alaska permanently. You know, live out at Glacier Point, help me run Wild Thing, maybe marry me...'

He'd run out of bravado, her stunned expression growing utterly still by the time he'd trailed off.

Not the best marriage proposal in the world, but he'd hedged his bets, leaving room to run if she thanked him again.

When she finally spoke, he braced himself.

'Did you just propose?'

'Sounded that way to me.'

He held his breath.

Then he saw it.

The first glimmer of warmth creeping into her eyes, the corners of her gorgeous mouth curving up, millimetre by millimetre.

'You'll have to do way better than that to convince me to live in your shack out in the sticks surrounded by all that ice.'

'I thought you liked my shack?'

She shrugged, mischief making her eyes twinkle. 'I do. And all those glaciers kind of grew on me too.'

She paused, tapped her lip. 'But there's my degree to consider—'

'Easy. You can study by correspondence.'

'Then there's the practical component of the course—'

'What could be better than hands-on experience with the world's best?'

A faint pink stained her cheeks as she glanced at him from beneath her lashes. 'That sounded very cocky.'

He laughed. 'I was talking about Wild Thing, but if you were referring to my hands-on expertise in other areas I'd be only too happy to—'

'Later.'

She placed her fingers over his lips, silencing him, her smile fading.

'I think it's great you've come all this way and been so honest with me, so I guess I owe you that much in return.'

Oh-oh. He didn't like the sound of this. Sounded like a prelude to a brush-off speech.

But what could he do? He'd confessed his feelings, pleaded his case, asked her to marry him. Him, the guy who'd made running away into an art. No way could he run with a wife, and, later, kids. Didn't she see that?

'I love you too. Probably fell in love with you way back when you spent your whole time running from me.'

Elated, he reached for her but she held him at bay. 'But are you sure all this isn't another form of escapism?'

His joy fizzled. 'What do you mean?'

She plucked at the parka's cord, fiddling, buying time, before she finally looked him in the eye.

'You had me before. You didn't want me. Now you don't have me, you want me. Have you stopped to consider this is a case of escaping what you currently have because it's old, trite, too comfortable, and wanting to always try something new?'

She paused, her expression solemn. 'Isn't it what you've always done?'

'No, of course not…'

He trailed off, all too aware she had a point.

Understanding shone in her eyes, her smile compassionate. But he didn't want her compassion, damn it, he wanted her. All of her. All the time.

How could he make her understand?

Yeah, he'd spent a lifetime running, but he'd change it all in an instant for a chance at spending the rest of his days with her.

'It's okay, I get it.' She patted his arm, like a mum comforting a kid, and he bristled. 'It's what you do, what you've always done. But I'm not willing to take a chance on a guy who could up and leave any time once he has me.'

'That would never happen,' he said through gritted teeth, knowing what it would take to convince her but hating to dredge up a past he'd so successfully buried.

She shook her head and when she finally met his gaze he saw pity.

'Look at your track record. Speaks for itself.'

He muttered a curse, attempted to drag a hand through his hair, the bulky glove infuriating him further. Ripping the gloves off, he flung them away, oblivious to the cold, oblivious to anything but convincing her they had a future.

'There's a reason I run.'

'Yeah, I know, Claudia—'

'No, before that.'

Pain ripped through him, as fresh and debilitating as the day he'd heard the news.

He hated feeling like this: so helpless, so out of control, so guilty. Guilty that Archie, the golden boy of the family, had died so young while he'd spent most of his life living the dream. Travelling the world, indulging his passion for nature, coasting from one job to another until making a huge success out of Wild Thing.

He'd done it all while his big, bold, boisterous brother had been taken too soon.

It wasn't fair.

'Rhys?'

Jade's tentative touch centred him. He had to get through this, had to tell her everything, for both their sakes.

'My eldest brother Archie was killed in a car accident when I was a kid.'

Sorrow down-turned her mouth. 'I'm so sorry.'

She captured his hand between her bulky gloves, squeezed it before releasing.

'You've met Callum. He coped by assuming Archie's position in the family firm. He was nineteen.'

Her eyebrows shot up and he nodded. 'Yeah, a joke. But he felt responsible, carried around this huge guilt because Archie had been on the way to pick him up from the cops. Just juvenile stuff, drunk and disorderly, but Callum paid for that night for years.'

'How?'

'Threw himself into the business twenty-four-seven. Didn't have time for anyone or anything else. Almost imploded.'

'What happened to him?'

Some of the pain eased as he recalled the phone call Callum had made to announce his engagement to Starr. He'd never heard him sound so upbeat.

'He met a woman and he changed.'

She could see where he was heading with this; he saw it in the sudden wariness around her eyes.

'Me, I coped by running away. Our parents only ever paid attention to Archie and when he died Callum and I became redundant. They blamed Callum and barely acknowledged I existed. So once I turned eighteen, I hit the road.'

'And you've been running ever since…'

'Yep.' He inhaled, pinched the bridge of his nose, and continued the confession that would hopefully convince her he meant every word. 'Then Claudia rocked up and I let her get close, the first person since Archie.'

Jade's mouth drooped. 'How involved were you?'

'We had a thing for a while.'

When her lips down-turned further, he rushed on. 'You know she was a daredevil—we had that in common. The adrenalin rush, the exhilaration, it was heady stuff, 'til I realised what we were doing was crazy. Then Claudia wanted to get serious and I backed off.'

He'd often wondered if he'd done things differently if she'd still have been alive. It had haunted him, her wounded expression turning defiant, a real 'I'll show you' smirk.

'She grew wilder, trying to keep me interested and I continued to cool things. Then I broke it off…'

The ever-present guilt lodged deep in his conscience jabbed him, hard. 'And that was the day she died.'

'Oh, my.'

Jade's hand flew to her mouth, her sympathy doing little to soothe him.

'Heading out to that glacier was her way of getting my attention, of keeping me interested despite what I'd said. And it ultimately got her killed.'

'That's why you blame yourself.'

He nodded. 'If I hadn't treated her like that, who knows—?'

'You said it yourself. She was a daredevil. You didn't force her to do anything. By the sounds of it, you reined her in, but she still had to push the boundaries.'

She reached a hesitant hand out to him, touched his sleeve. 'You've got to let this go before it eats you up inside.'

Regretting when she dropped her hand, he went for broke. 'Want to know the silly part? When I saw you pushing yourself harder to meet my expectations, saw you trying new things without a qualm, you reminded me of her in a way and I used that as some warped justification to push you away. When in fact you're nothing like her.'

A wry smile twisted her mouth. 'Good to hear.'

'Even with Claudia, I wanted to keep running and not look back. I've always run. It's what I do.'

Stepping into her personal space, he trailed a fingertip down her cheek. 'Until now.'

Her bottom lip quivered and he rushed on. 'All this time I've been petrified of staying in one spot too long, getting too attached to anything.'

Cupping her chin, he tilted it up gently. 'But you know something? Some things are just worth the risk.'

Before she could react he kissed her with all the pent-up passion and frustration and hope that had been driving him mad.

He'd missed her so much, had never imagined in his wildest dreams he'd crave someone so much.

She hesitated for a fraction of a second before flinging her arms around his waist and kissing him as if she'd missed him right back.

When she sagged against him and the backs of his knees bumped the ice couch, he eased off.

'Whoa! Landing on a sofa with you on top of me would normally be appealing, but on that?'

He winced. 'I think we need to both be in one piece to celebrate our future properly.'

The corners of her eyes crinkled adorably. 'So you think I'm going to go for your plan, huh?'

'After I've bared my soul to you? Professed my undying love? Travelled around the world to prove it? Arranged all this—'

'Okay, okay.' She laughed, a joyous sound that echoed off the walls. 'Yeah, I happen to think your plan is a good one.'

Holding her close, he nuzzled her neck. 'Which part?'

'All of it.'

He pulled back, searched her face for confirmation. 'You mean—'

'We're getting married and we'll live at Glacier Point and I'll run Wild Thing with you and study by correspondence. Happy?'

He let out a loud whoop and spun her around until they were both breathless and laughing.

When they finally stopped, their parka zips had tangled and no amount of jiggling could release them.

'Fate?'

He growled, renewed his efforts to free them. 'Maybe. But you've got on too many clothes for what I have in mind.'

'In here? Are you nuts?'

'About you.'

He swooped in for another kiss as the zips gave and, despite his best efforts to stay upright, they fell onto the ice couch.

'Ouch!'

He righted her, patted her down to check for injuries. Any excuse.

'You landed on me and you're complaining?'

In response, she wriggled in his lap and suddenly his butt wasn't the only thing aching down there.

'My hero.'

She batted her eyelashes at him and his heart gave a funny twinge at her antics. The same odd gripe since he'd let this special woman into his life.

'And don't you forget it.'

This time, their kiss packed enough sizzle to melt the entire room.

Neither cared.

EPILOGUE

Jade's breath caught as she stared at the glacier in awe. She never tired of its majestic beauty and, though she'd seen it a hundred times over the last six months, every time was like the first.

'What are you thinking?'

She gazed up at her gorgeous husband, rivalling the glacier in the stunning stakes.

'Remember the first time you brought me here? The canoe and how we almost took a dunking?'

He laughed, a rich, vibrant sound that still had the power to reduce her insides to mush.

'How could I forget? Funnily enough, I thought about jumping into that lake myself many times over the succeeding months. Anything to cool me down after facing the temptress you were. You drove me crazy, you know that?'

'Drove? As in past tense?'

In response he crushed her lips beneath his, his kiss flooding her body with heat and sizzle and need.

'Does that answer your question?' he whispered against the side of her mouth.

At that moment a distant roar quickly turned thunderously loud.

'Quick, look!'

He pointed at the glacier as a monstrous chunk of ice cleaved off the cliff face.

'Wow…'

In all her time here she hadn't seen the famed ice calving

she'd heard so much about and witnessing nature's grand display brought a lump to her throat.

Slipping his arms around her waist, she leaned back against him, his familiar, solid heat a comfort as always.

'You're awfully quiet.'

He brushed a kiss across her hair and she turned her head slightly, glanced up.

'We're two of the luckiest people on this planet,' she said, tears of happiness stinging her eyes as his love for her shone clearly, rivalling the myriad rainbow colours over Davidson Glacier in its brilliance.

'Yeah, we are.'

'Uncle Re-e-e-s! We can see you!'

'Sprung,' he muttered as she laughed and slipped out of his arms in time to catch one of the twins barrelling towards them.

'Hey, you guys, you just missed an ice calving.'

Polly, a precocious three year old, whispered loudly in her brother's ear. 'That's silly. Only cows have calves.'

Squatting to the kids' level, Rhys hugged them both close. 'You know what? I reckon we should celebrate this occasion with some ice…cream! What do you say?'

Screams of 'yay!' filled the air as the lump in Jade's throat expanded.

Rhys was so great with kids. She couldn't wait to finish her degree and get started on another pressing project: adding to their family.

As Rhys tussled with the kids Callum and Starr arrived.

'You missed—'

Callum smirked. 'We didn't miss it. We saw you two—'

Starr elbowed Callum. 'And thought you deserved some privacy.'

'Thanks.'

Callum jerked his thumb at the twins. 'Try restraining those two. No mean feat, let me tell you.'

Jade smiled as Starr glanced at her kids, maternal pride adding to the perpetual glow the beautiful dancer had.

'Rhys seems to be doing a fair job now.'

'That's because he gets to spoil them and play the generous uncle while I—'

'Spoil them just as much.' Starr rolled her eyes. 'These Cartwright guys are putty in the right hands.'

Rhys glanced up at that moment and their gazes locked, Jade's heart instantly jackknifing. 'Tell me about it.'

With a fond grin at his wife, Callum shouted out, 'Hey, Rhys. These two are ganging up on us.'

Rhys laughed. 'Again?'

Polly tugged on Rhys's hand. 'I'm starving!'

Hamish joined the cry. 'Me too!'

'Salmon steaks for everyone.' Jade slipped her hand into Rhys's as the twins scampered ahead on the trail and Callum and Starr brought up the rear.

'I like this place,' Callum said, his teasing tone alerting her to another incoming brotherly missile. 'Even a drifter like you can make a home with the right woman.'

'Right back at you, bro.'

Rhys cocked his hand and made a firing gun sign as the brothers laughed.

Starr shrugged, smiled in a 'what are we going to do with these bozos?' grin.

Jade knew what she'd like to do with her husband, and as they reached the house he pulled her off to the side while Callum, Starr and the twins continued on.

'Callum's right. While I love this place, always have, you're home to me.'

A second before his lips met hers, she whispered, 'Right back at you.'

Harlequin *Presents*

Coming Next Month

from **Harlequin Presents®**. Available May 31, 2011.

Coming Next Month

from **Harlequin Presents® EXTRA**. Available June 14, 2011.

Visit www.HarlequinInsideRomance.com
for more information on upcoming titles!

HPECNM0511

REQUEST YOUR
FREE BOOKS!

◆Harlequin *Presents*

2 FREE NOVELS PLUS
2 FREE GIFTS!

PASSION GUARANTEED SEDUCTION

YES! Please send me 2 FREE Harlequin Presents® novels and my 2 FREE gifts (gifts are worth about $10). After receiving them, if I don't wish to receive any more books, I can return the shipping statement marked "cancel." If I don't cancel, I will receive 6 brand-new novels every month and be billed just $4.05 per book in the U.S. or $4.74 per book in Canada. That's a saving of at least 15% off the cover price! It's quite a bargain! Shipping and handling is just 50¢ per book in the U.S. and 75¢ per book in Canada.* I understand that accepting the 2 free books and gifts places me under no obligation to buy anything. I can always return a shipment and cancel at any time. Even if I never buy another book, the two free books and gifts are mine to keep forever.   106/306 HDN FC55

Name	(PLEASE PRINT)

Address	Apt. #

City	State/Prov.	Zip/Postal Code

Signature (if under 18, a parent or guardian must sign)

Mail to the **Reader Service:**
IN U.S.A.: P.O. Box 1867, Buffalo, NY 14240-1867
IN CANADA: P.O. Box 609, Fort Erie, Ontario L2A 5X3

Not valid for current subscribers to Harlequin Presents books.

**Are you a current subscriber to Harlequin Presents books
and want to receive the larger-print edition?
Call 1-800-873-8635 or visit www.ReaderService.com.**

* Terms and prices subject to change without notice. Prices do not include applicable taxes. Sales tax applicable in N.Y. Canadian residents will be charged applicable taxes. Offer not valid in Quebec. This offer is limited to one order per household. All orders subject to credit approval. Credit or debit balances in a customer's account(s) may be offset by any other outstanding balance owed by or to the customer. Please allow 4 to 6 weeks for delivery. Offer available while quantities last.

Your Privacy—The Reader Service is committed to protecting your privacy. Our Privacy Policy is available online at www.ReaderService.com or upon request from the Reader Service.

We make a portion of our mailing list available to reputable third parties that offer products we believe may interest you. If you prefer that we not exchange your name with third parties, or if you wish to clarify or modify your communication preferences, please visit us at www.ReaderService.com/consumerschoice or write to us at Reader Service Preference Service, P.O. Box 9062, Buffalo, NY 14269. Include your complete name and address.

Harlequin® Blaze™ brings you
New York Times *and* USA TODAY *bestselling author*
Vicki Lewis Thompson with three new steamy titles
from the bestselling miniseries SONS OF CHANCE

Chance isn't just the last name of these rugged
Wyoming cowboys—it's their motto, too!

Read on for a sneak peek at the first title,
SHOULD'VE BEEN A COWBOY

Available June 2011 only from Harlequin® Blaze™.

"THANKS FOR NOT TURNING ON THE LIGHTS," Tyler said. "I'm a mess."

"Not in my book." Even in low light, Alex had a good view of her yellow shirt plastered to her body. It was all he could do not to reach for her, mud and all. But the next move needed to be hers, not his.

She slicked her wet hair back and squeezed some water out of the ends as she glanced upward. "I like the sound of the rain on a tin roof."

"Me, too."

She met his gaze briefly and looked away. "Where's the sink?"

"At the far end, beyond the last stall."

Tyler's running shoes squished as she walked down the aisle between the rows of stalls. She glanced sideways at Alex. "So how much of a cowboy are you these days? Do you ride the range and stuff?"

"I ride." He liked being able to say that. "Why?"

"Just wondered. Last summer, you were still a city boy. You even told me you weren't the cowboy type, but you're…different now."

He wasn't sure if that was a good thing or a bad thing. Maybe she preferred city boys to cowboys. "How am I different?"

"Well, you dress differently, and your hair's a little longer. Your face seems a little more chiseled, but maybe that's because of your hair. Also, there's something else, something harder to define, an attitude…"

"Are you saying I have an attitude?"

"Not in a bad way. It's more like a quiet confidence."

He was flattered, but still he had to laugh. "I just admitted a while ago that I have all kinds of doubts about this event tomorrow. That doesn't seem like quiet confidence to me."

"This isn't about your job, it's about…your…" She took a deep breath. "It's about your sex appeal, okay? I have no business talking about it, because it will only make me want to do things I shouldn't do." She started toward the end of the barn. "Now, where's that sink? We need to get cleaned up and go back to the house. Dinner is probably ready, and I—"

He spun her around and pulled her into his arms, mud and all. "Let's do those things." Then he kissed her, knowing that she would kiss him back, knowing that this time he would take that kiss where he wanted it to go. And she would let him.

Follow Tyler and Alex's wild adventures in
SHOULD'VE BEEN A COWBOY
Available June 2011 only from Harlequin® Blaze™
wherever books are sold.

Harlequin Presents®

brings you

USA TODAY *bestselling author*

Lucy Monroe

*with her new installment
in the much-loved miniseries*

Royal Brides

**Proud, passionate rulers—
marriage is by royal decree!**

Meet Zahir and Asad—two powerful, brooding sheikhs
and masters of all they survey. They need brides,
and marriage in their kingdoms is by royal decree!

Capture a slice of royal life in this enthralling sheikh saga!

Coming in June 2011:
FOR DUTY'S SAKE

**Available wherever
Harlequin Presents® books are sold.**

HP12993